PRIVATE PEACEFUL

PRIVATE PEACEFUL

MICHAEL MORPURGO

SCHOLASTIC PRESS

NEW YORK

LIBRARY OF CONGRESS CATALOGING-IN-PUBLICATION DATA
Morpurgo, Michael. Private Peaceful / by Michael Morpurgo.—1st American ed p.   cm. Summary: When Thomas Peaceful's older brother is forced to join the British Army, Thomas decides to sign up as well, although he is only fourteen years old, to prove himself to his country, his family, his childhood love, Molly, and himself. ISBN 0-439-63648-5 (alk. paper)—ISBN 0-439-63652-1 (pb. : alk. paper) [1. Single-parent families—Fiction.   2. Poverty—Fiction.   3. Soldiers—Fiction. 4. People with mental disabilities—Fiction.   5. World War, 1914–1918—England—Fiction. 6. Great Britain—History—George V, 1910–1936—Fiction.]   I. Title.
PZ7.M82712Pr 2004   [Fic]—dc22   2003065347

10 9 8 7 6 5 4 3   05 06 07 08

Printed in the United States of America   37
First American edition, October 2004
The text type was set in Adobe Caslon.
Book design by David Caplan

For my dear godmother,

Mary Niven

FIVE PAST TEN

They've gone now, and I'm alone at last. I have the whole night ahead of me, and I won't waste a single moment of it. I shan't sleep it away. I won't dream it away either. I mustn't, because every moment of it will be far too precious.

I want to try to remember everything, just as it was, just as it happened. I've had nearly eighteen years of yesterdays and tomorrows, and tonight I must remember as many of them as I can. I want tonight to be long, as long as my life, not filled with fleeting dreams that rush me on towards dawn.

Tonight, more than any other night of my life, I want to feel alive.

❖   ❖   ❖

Charlie is taking me by the hand, leading me because he knows I don't want to go. I've never worn a collar before and it's choking me. My boots are strange and heavy on my feet. My heart is heavy too, because I dread what I am going to. Charlie has told me often how terrible this school-place is: about Mr. Munnings and his raging tempers and the long whipping cane he hangs on the wall above his desk.

Big Joe doesn't have to go to school and I don't think that's fair at all. He's much older than me. He's even older than Charlie and he's never been to school. He stays at home with Mother, and sits up in his tree singing *Oranges and Lemons*, and laughing. Big Joe is always happy, always laughing. I wish I could be happy like him. I wish I could be at home like him. I don't want to go with Charlie. I don't want to go to school.

I look back, over my shoulder, hoping for a reprieve, hoping that Mother will come running after me and take me home. But she doesn't come and she doesn't come, and school and Mr. Munnings and his cane are getting closer with every step.

"Piggyback?" says Charlie. He sees my eyes full of tears

and knows how it is. Charlie always knows how it is. He's three years older than me, so he's done everything and knows everything. He's strong too, and very good at piggybacks. So I hop up and cling on tight, crying behind my closed eyes, trying not to whimper out loud. But I cannot hold back my sobbing for long because I know that this morning is not the beginning of anything — not new and exciting as Mother says it is — but rather the end of my beginning. Clinging on round Charlie's neck I know that I am living the last moments of my carefree time, that I will not be the same person when I come home this afternoon.

I open my eyes and see a dead crow hanging from the fence, his beak open. Was he shot, shot in mid-scream, as he began to sing, his raucous tune scarcely begun? He sways, his feathers still catching the wind even in death, his family and friends cawing in their grief and anger from the high elm trees above us. I am not sorry for him. It could be him that drove away my robin and emptied her nest of her eggs. My eggs. Five of them there had been, live and warm under my fingers. I remember I took them out one by one and laid them in the palm of my hand. I wanted them for my tin, to blow them like Charlie did and lay them in cotton wool with my blackbird's eggs and my pigeon's eggs. I would have taken them. But something made me draw back, made me hesitate.

3

The robin was watching me from Father's rose bush, her black and beady eyes unblinking, begging me.

Father was in that bird's eyes. Under the rose bush, deep down, buried in the damp and wormy earth were all his precious things. Mother had put his pipe in first. Then Charlie laid his hobnail boots side by side, curled into each other, sleeping. Big Joe knelt down and covered the boots in Father's old scarf.

"Your turn, Tommo," Mother said. But I couldn't bring myself to do it. I was holding the gloves he'd worn the morning he died. I remembered picking one of them up. I knew what they did not know, what I could never tell them.

Mother helped me to do it in the end, so that Father's gloves lay there on top of his scarf, palms uppermost, thumbs touching. I felt those hands willing me not to do it, willing me to think again, not to take the eggs, not to take what was not mine. So I didn't do it. Instead I watched them grow, saw the first scrawny skeletal stirrings, the nest of gaping, begging beaks, the frenzied screeching at feeding time; witnessed too late from my bedroom window the last of the early-morning massacre, the parent robins watching like me, distraught and helpless, while the marauding crows made off skywards cackling, their murderous deed done. I don't like crows. I've never liked crows. That crow hanging there on the fence got what he deserved. That's what I think.

Charlie is finding the hill up into the village hard going. I can see the church tower and below it the roof of the school. My mouth is dry with fear. I cling on tighter.

"First day's the worst, Tommo," Charlie's saying, breathing hard. "It's not so bad. Honest." Whenever Charlie says "honest," I know it's not true. "Anyway I'll look after you."

That I do believe, because he always has. He does look after me too, setting me down, and walking me through all the boisterous banter of the school yard, his hand on my shoulder, comforting me, protecting me.

The school bell rings and we line up in two silent rows, about twenty children in each. I recognize some of them from Sunday school. I look around and realize that Charlie is no longer beside me. He's in the other line, and he's winking at me. I blink back and he laughs. I can't wink with one eye, not yet. Charlie always thinks that's very funny. Then I see Mr. Munnings standing on the school steps cracking his knuckles in the suddenly silent school yard. He has tufty cheeks and a big belly under his waistcoat. He has a gold watch open in his hand. It's his eyes that are frightening and I know they are searching me out.

"Aha!" he cries, pointing right at me. Everyone has turned to look. "A new boy, a new boy to add to my trials and tribulations. Was not one Peaceful enough? What have I done to deserve another one? First a Charlie Peaceful, and now a Thomas Peaceful. Is there no end to my woes? Understand this, Thomas Peaceful, that here I am your lord and master. You do what I say when I say it. You do not cheat, you do not lie, you do not blaspheme. You do not come to school in bare feet. And your hands will be clean. These are my commandments. Do I make myself absolutely clear?"

"Yes sir," I whisper, surprised I can find my voice at all.

We file in past him, hands behind our backs. Charlie smiles across at me as the two lines part: "Tiddlers" into my classroom, "Bigguns" into his. I'm the littlest of the Tiddlers. Most of the Bigguns are even bigger than Charlie, fourteen years old some of them. I watch him until the door closes behind him and he's gone. Until this moment I have never known what it is to feel truly alone.

My bootlaces are undone. I can't tie laces. Charlie can, but he's not here. I hear Mr. Munnings' thunderous voice next door calling the roll and I am so glad we have Miss McAllister. She may speak with a strange accent, but at least she smiles, and at least she's not Mr. Munnings.

"Thomas," she tells me, "you will be sitting there, next to Molly. And your laces are undone."

Everyone seems to be tittering at me as I take my place. All I want to do is to escape, to run, but I don't dare do it. All I can do is cry. I hang my head so they can't see my tears coming.

"Crying won't do your laces up, you know," Miss McAllister says.

"I can't, Miss," I tell her.

"Can't is not a word we use in my class, Thomas Peaceful," she says. "We shall just have to teach you to tie your boot-laces. That's what we're all here for, Thomas, to learn. That's why we come to school, don't we? You show him, Molly. Molly's the oldest girl in my class, Thomas, and my best pupil. She'll help you."

So while she calls the roll Molly kneels down in front of me and does up my laces. She ties laces very differently from Charlie, delicately, more slowly, in a great loopy double knot. She doesn't look up at me while she's doing it, not once, and I wish she would. She has hair the same color as Billyboy, Father's old horse — chestnut brown and shining — and I want to reach out and touch it. Then she looks up at me at last and smiles. It's all I need. Suddenly I no longer want to run home. I want to stay here with Molly. I know I have a friend.

In playtime, in the school yard, I want to go over and talk to her, but I can't because she's always surrounded by a gaggle of giggling girls. They keep looking at me over their shoulders and laughing. I look for Charlie, but Charlie's splitting conkers open with his friends, all of them Bigguns. I go to sit on an old tree stump. I undo my bootlaces and try to do them up again remembering how Molly did it. I try again and again. After only a short while I find I can do it. It's untidy, and it's loose, but I can do it. Best of all, from across the school yard Molly sees I can do it, and smiles at me.

At home we don't wear boots, except for church. Mother does of course, and Father always wore his great hobnail boots, the boots he died in. When the tree came down I was there in the wood with him, just the two of us. Before I ever went to school he'd often take me off to work with him, to keep me out of mischief, he said. I'd ride up behind him on Billyboy and hang on round his waist, my face pressed into his back. Whenever Billyboy broke into a gallop I'd love it. We galloped all the way that morning, up the hill, up through Ford's Cleave Wood. I was still giggling when he lifted me down.

"Off you go, you scallywag, you," he said. "Enjoy yourself."

I hardly needed to be told. There were badger holes and fox holes to peer into, deer prints to follow perhaps, flowers to pick, or butterflies to chase. But that morning I found a mouse,

8

a dead mouse. I buried it under a pile of leaves. I was making a wooden cross for it. Father was chopping away rhythmically nearby, grunting and groaning at every stroke as he always did. It sounded at first as if Father was just groaning a bit louder. That's what I thought it was. But then, strangely, the sound seemed to be coming not from where he was, but from somewhere high up in the branches.

I looked up to see the great tree above me swaying when all the other trees were standing still. It was creaking while all the other trees were silent. Only slowly did I realize it was coming down, and that when it fell it would fall right on top of me, that I was going to die and there was nothing I could do about it. I stood and stared, mesmerized at the gradual fall of it, my legs frozen under me, quite incapable of movement.

I hear Father shouting: "Tommo! Tommo! Run, Tommo!" But I can't. I see Father running towards me through the trees, his shirt flailing. I feel him catch me up and toss me aside in one movement, like a wheat sheaf. There is a roaring thunder in my ears and then no more.

When I wake I see Father at once, see the soles of his boots with their worn nails. I crawl over to where he is lying, pinned to the ground under the leafy crown of the great tree. He is on his back, his face turned away from me as if he doesn't want me to see. One arm is outstretched towards me, his glove fallen off, his finger pointing at me. There is blood coming from his nose, dropping on the leaves. His eyes are open, but I know at once they are not seeing me. He is not breathing. When I shout at him, when I shake him, he does not wake up. I pick up his glove.

In the church we're sitting side by side in the front row, Mother, Big Joe, Charlie and me. We've never in our lives sat in the front row before. It's where the Colonel and his family always sit. The coffin rests on trestles, my father inside in his Sunday suit. A swallow swoops over our heads all through the prayers, all through the hymns, flitting from window to window, from the belfry to the altar, looking for some way out. And I know for certain it is Father trying to escape. I know it because he told us more than once that in his next life he'd like to be a bird, so he could fly free wherever he wanted.

Big Joe keeps pointing up at the swallow. Then without any warning he gets up and walks to the back of the church where he opens the door. When he gets back he explains to Mother what he's done in his loud voice, and Grandma Wolf, sitting beside us in her black bonnet, scowls at him, at all of us. I know then what I never understood before, that she is ashamed to be one of us. I didn't really understand why until later, until I was older.

The swallow sits perched on a rafter high above the coffin. It lifts off and swoops up and down the aisle until at last it finds the open door and is gone. And I know that Father is happy now in his next life. Big Joe laughs out loud and Mother takes his hand in hers. Charlie catches my eye. At that moment all four of us are thinking the very same thing.

The Colonel gets up into the pulpit to speak, his hand clutching the lapel of his jacket. He declares that James Peaceful was a good man, one of the best workers he has ever known, the salt of the earth, always cheerful as he went about his work, that the Peaceful family had been employed in one capacity or another, by his family, for five generations. In all his thirty years as a forester on the estate James Peaceful had never once been late for work and was a credit to his family and his village. All the while as the Colonel drones on I'm thinking of the rude things Father used to say about him — "silly old fart," "mad old duffer" and much worse — and how Mother had always told us that he might well be a "silly old fart" or "mad old duffer," but how it was the Colonel who paid Father's wages and owned the roof over our heads, how we children should show respect when we met him, smile and touch our forelocks, and we should look as if we meant it too, if we knew what was good for us.

Afterwards we all gather round the grave and Father's lowered down, and the vicar won't stop talking. I want Father to hear the birds for the last time before the earth closes in on top of him and he has nothing left but silence. Father loves larks, loves watching them rising, rising so high you can only see their song. I look up hoping for a lark, and there is a blackbird singing from the yew tree. A blackbird will have to do . . . I hear Mother whispering to Big Joe that Father is not really in his coffin anymore, but in heaven up there — she's pointing up into the sky beyond the church tower — and that he's happy, happy as the birds.

The earth thuds and thumps down on the coffin behind us as we drift away, leaving him. We walk home together along the deep lanes, Big Joe plucking at the foxgloves and the honey-suckle, filling Mother's hands with flowers, and none of us has any tears to cry or words to say. Me least of all. For I have inside me a secret so horrible, a secret I can never tell anyone, not even Charlie. Father needn't have died that morning in Ford's Cleave Wood. He was trying to save me. If only I had tried to save myself, if I had run, he would not now be lying dead in his coffin. As Mother smooths my hair and Big Joe offers her yet another foxglove, all I can think is that I have caused this.

I have killed my own father.

TWENTY TO ELEVEN

I don't want to eat. Stew, potatoes and biscuits. I usually like stew, but I've no appetite for it. I nibble at a biscuit, but I don't want that either. Not now. It's a good thing Grandma Wolf is not here. She always hated us leaving food on our plates. "Waste not, want not," she'd say. I'm wasting this, Wolfwoman, whether you like it or not.

❖　❖　❖

Big Joe ate more than all the rest of us put together. Everything was his favorite — bread and butter pudding with

raisins, potato pie, cheese and pickle, stew and dumplings —
whatever Mother cooked, he'd stuff it in and scoff it down.
Anything Charlie and I didn't like we'd shuffle onto his plate
when Mother wasn't looking. Big Joe always loved the con-
spiracy of that, and he loved the extra food too. There was
nothing he wouldn't eat. When we were little, before we knew
better, Charlie once bet me an owl's skull I'd found that Big
Joe would even eat rabbit droppings. I couldn't believe he
would, because I thought Big Joe must know what they were.
So I took the bet. Charlie put a handful of them in a paper
bag and told him they were sweets. Big Joe took them out of
the bag and popped them into his mouth, savoring every one
of them. And when we laughed, he laughed too and offered
us one each. But Charlie said they were especially for him,
a present. I thought Big Joe might get ill after that, but he
never did.

Mother told us when we were older that Big Joe had
nearly died just a few days after he was born. Meningitis, they
told her at the hospital. The doctor said Joe had brain damage,
that he'd be no use to anyone, even if he lived. But Big Joe did
live, and he did get better, though never completely. As we
were growing up, all we knew was that he was different. It
didn't matter to us that he couldn't speak very well, that he
couldn't read or write at all, that he didn't think like we did,

like other people did. To us he was just Big Joe. He did frighten us sometimes. He seemed to drift off to live in a dream world of his own, often a world of nightmares I thought because he could become very agitated and upset. But sooner or later he always came back to us and would be himself again, the Big Joe we all knew, the Big Joe who loved everything and everyone, especially animals and birds and flowers, totally trusting, always forgiving — even when he found out that his sweets were rabbit droppings.

Charlie and I got into real trouble over that. Big Joe would never have found out, not by himself. But, always generous, he went and offered one of the rabbit droppings to Mother. She was so angry with us I thought she'd burst. She put a finger in Big Joe's mouth, scooped out what was still in there and made him wash it out. Then she made Charlie and me eat one rabbit dropping each so that we'd know what it was like.

"Horrible, isn't it?" she said. "Horrible food for horrible children. Don't you treat Big Joe like that ever again."

We felt very ashamed of ourselves — for a while anyway. Ever since then someone has only had to mention rabbits, for Charlie and me to smile at one another and remember. It's making me smile again now, even just thinking of it. It shouldn't, but it does.

In a way our lives at home always revolved around Big Joe. How we thought about people depended largely on how they behaved with our big brother. It was quite simple really: If people didn't like him or were offhand or treated him as if he was stupid, then we didn't like them. Most people around us were used to him, but some would look the other way, or worse still, just pretend he wasn't there. We hated that more than anything. Big Joe never seemed to mind, but we did on his behalf — like the day we blew raspberries at the Colonel.

No one at home ever spoke well of the Colonel, except Grandma Wolf, of course. Whenever she came for her visits she wouldn't hear a word against him. She and Father would have dreadful rows about him. We grew up thinking of him mostly as just a "silly old fart." But the first time I saw for myself what the Colonel was really like, was because of Big Joe.

One evening Charlie and Big Joe and I were coming back home up the lane. We'd been fishing for brown trout in the brook. Big Joe had caught three, tickled them to sleep in the shallows and then scooped them out onto the bank before they knew what had happened. He was clever like that. It was almost as if he knew what the fish were thinking. He never liked killing them though, and nor did I. Charlie had to do that.

Big Joe always said hello, loudly, to everyone. It's how he

was. So when the Colonel rode by that evening, Big Joe called out hello, and proudly held up his trout to show him. The Colonel trotted by as if he hadn't even seen us. When he'd passed Charlie blew a noisy raspberry after him, and Big Joe did the same because he liked rude noises. But the trouble was that Big Joe was enjoying himself so much blowing raspberries that he didn't stop. The Colonel reined in his horse and gave us a very nasty look. For a moment I thought he was going to come after us. Luckily he didn't, but he did crack his whip. "I'll teach you, you young ruffians!" he roared. "I'll teach you!"

I've always thought that was the moment the Colonel began to hate us, that from then on he was always determined one way or another to get his own back. We ran for it all the way home. Whenever anyone farts or blows raspberries I always think of that meeting in the lane, of how Big Joe always laughs at rude noises, laughs like he'll never stop. I think too, of the menacing look in the Colonel's eye and the crack of his whip, and how Big Joe blowing raspberries at him that evening may well have changed our lives for ever.

It was Big Joe, too, who got me into my first fight. There was a lot of fighting at school, but I was never much good at it and always seemed to end up getting a swollen lip or a bleeding ear. I learned soon enough that if you don't want to get hurt you keep your head down and you don't answer back, particularly if the other fellow is bigger. But one day I discovered that sometimes you've got to stand up for yourself and fight for what's right, even when you don't want to.

It was at playtime. Big Joe came up to school to see Charlie and me. He just stood and watched us from outside the school gate. He did that often when Charlie and I first went off to school together — I think he was finding it lonely at home without us. I ran over to him. He was breathless, bright-eyed with excitement. He had something to show me. He opened his cupped hands just enough for me to be able to see. There was a slowworm curled up inside. I knew where he'd got it from — the churchyard, his favorite hunting ground. Whenever we went up to put flowers on Father's grave, Big Joe would go off on his own, hunting for more creatures to add to his collection; that's when he wasn't just standing there gazing up at the tower and singing *Oranges and Lemons* at the top of his voice and watching the swifts screaming around the church tower. Nothing seemed to make him happier than that.

I knew Big Joe would put his slowworm in with all his other creatures. He kept them in boxes at the back of the woodshed at home — lizards, hedgehogs, all sorts. I stroked his slowworm with my finger, and said it was lovely, which it was. Then he wandered off, walking down the lane humming his *Oranges and Lemons* as he went, gazing down in wonder at his beloved slowworm.

I am watching him go when someone taps me hard on my shoulder, hard enough to hurt. It is big Jimmy Parsons. Charlie has often warned me about him, told me to keep out of his way. "Who's got a loony for a brother?" says Jimmy Parsons, sneering at me.

I cannot believe what he's said, not at first. "What did you say?"

"Your brother's a loony, off his head, off his rocker, nuts, barmy."

I go for him then, fists flailing, screaming at him, but I don't manage to land a single punch. He hits me full in the face and sends me sprawling. I find myself suddenly sitting on the ground, wiping my bleeding nose and looking at the blood on the back of my hand. Then he puts the boot in, hard. I curl up in a ball like a hedgehog to protect myself, but it doesn't seem to do me much good. He just goes on kicking me on my back, on my legs, anywhere he can. When he finally stops I wonder why.

I look up to see Charlie grabbing him round the neck and pulling him to the ground. They're rolling over and over, punching each other and swearing. The whole school has gathered round to watch now, egging them on. That's when Mr. Munnings comes running out of the school, roaring like a raging bull. He pulls them apart, takes them by their collars and drags them off inside the school. Luckily for me Mr. Munnings never even notices me sitting there, bleeding. Charlie gets the cane, and so does Jimmy Parsons — six strokes each. So Charlie saves me twice that day. The rest of us stand there in the school yard in silence, listening to the strokes and counting them. Big Jimmy Parsons gets it first, and he keeps crying out: "Ow, sir! Ow, sir! Ow, sir!" But when it's Charlie's turn, all we hear are the whacks, and then the silences in between. I am so proud of him for that. I have the bravest brother in the world.

Molly comes over and, taking me by the hand, leads me towards the pump. She soaks her handkerchief under it and dabs my nose and my hands and my knee — the blood seems to be everywhere. The water is wonderfully cold and soothing, and her hands are soft. She doesn't say anything for a while. She's dabbing me very gently, very carefully so as not to hurt me. Then all of a sudden she says: "I like Big Joe. He's kind. I like people who are kind."

Molly likes Big Joe. Now I know for sure that I will love her till the day I die.

After a while Charlie came out into the school yard hitching up his trousers and grinning in the sunshine. Everyone was crowding around him.

"Did it hurt, Charlie?"

"Was it on the back of the knees, Charlie, or on your bum?"

Charlie never said a word to them. He just walked right through everyone, and came straight over to me and Molly. "He won't do it again, Tommo," he said. "I hit him where it hurts, in the goolies." He lifted my chin and peered at my nose. "Are you all right, Tommo?"

"Hurts a bit," I told him.

"So does my bum," said Charlie.

Molly laughed then, and so did I. So did Charlie, and so did the whole school.

From that moment on Molly became one of us. It was as if she had suddenly joined our family and become our sister. When Molly came home with us that afternoon Big Joe gave her some flowers he'd picked, and Mother treated her like the daughter she'd never had. After that, Molly came home with us almost every afternoon. She seemed to want to be with us all the time. We didn't discover the reason for this until a lot later. I remember Mother used to brush Molly's hair. She loved doing it and we loved watching.

Mother. I think of her so often. And when I think of her I think of high hedges and deep lanes and our walks down to the river together in the evenings. I think of meadowsweet and honeysuckle and vetch and foxgloves and red campion and dog roses. There wasn't a wild flower or a butterfly she couldn't name. I loved the sound of their names when she spoke them: red admiral, peacock, cabbage white, adonis blue. It's her voice I'm hearing in my head now. I don't know why, but I can hear her better than I can picture her. I suppose it was because of Big Joe that she was always talking, always explaining the world about us. She was his guide, his interpreter, his teacher.

They wouldn't have Big Joe at school. Mr. Munnings said he was backward. He wasn't backward at all. He was different, "special" Mother used to call him, but he was not backward. He needed help, that's all, and Mother was his help. It was as if Big Joe was blind in some way. He could see perfectly well, but very often he didn't seem to understand what he was seeing. And he wanted to understand so badly. So Mother would be forever telling him how and why things were as they were. And she would sing to him often, too, because it always made him happy and soothed him whenever he had one of his turns and became anxious or troubled. She'd sing to Charlie and me as well, more out of habit, I think. But we loved it, loved the sound of her voice. Her voice was the music of our childhood.

After Father died the music stopped. There was a stillness and a quietness in Mother now, and a sadness about the house. I had my terrible secret, a secret I could scarcely ever put out of my mind. So in my guilt I kept more and more to myself. Even Big Joe hardly ever laughed. At meals the kitchen seemed especially empty without Father, without his bulk and his voice filling the room. His dirty work coat didn't hang on the porch any more, and the smell of his pipe lingered only faintly now. He was gone and we were all quietly mourning him in our way.

Mother still talked to Big Joe, but not as much as before. She had to talk to him, because she was the only one who truly understood the meaning of all the grunts and squawks Big Joe used for language. Charlie and I understood some of it, some of the time, but she seemed to understand all he wanted to say, sometimes even before he said it. There was a shadow hanging over her, Charlie and I could see that, and not only the shadow of Father's death. We were sure there was something else she wouldn't talk about, something she was hiding from us. We found out what it was only too soon.

We were back home after school having our tea — Molly was there too — when there was a knock on the door. Mother seemed at once to know who it was. She took time to gather herself, smoothing down her apron and arranging her hair before she opened the door. It was the Colonel. "I wanted a word, Mrs. Peaceful," he said. "I think you know what I've come for."

Mother told us to finish our tea, closed the door and went out into the garden with him. Charlie and I left Molly and Big Joe at the table and dashed out of the back door. We hurdled the vegetables, ran along the hedge, crouched down behind the woodshed and listened. We were close enough to hear every word that was said.

"It may seem a little indelicate to broach the subject so soon after your late husband's sad and untimely death," the Colonel was saying. He wasn't looking at Mother as he spoke, but down at his top hat which he was smoothing with his sleeve. "But it's a question of the cottage. Strictly speaking, of course, Mrs. Peaceful, you have no right to live here any more. You know well enough I think that this is a tied cottage, tied to your late husband's job on the estate. Now of course with him gone . . ."

"I know what you're saying, Colonel," Mother said. "You want us out."

"Well, I wouldn't put it quite like that. It's not that I want you out, Mrs. Peaceful, not if we can come to some other arrangement."

"Arrangement? What arrangement?" Mother asked.

"Well," the Colonel went on, "as it happens there's a position up at the house that might suit you. My wife's lady's maid has just given notice. As you know my wife is not a well woman. These days she spends most of her life in a wheelchair. She needs constant care and attention seven days a week."

"But I have my children," Mother protested. "Who would look after my children?"

It was a while before the Colonel spoke. "The two boys are old enough now to fend for themselves, I should have thought. And as for the other one, there is the lunatic asylum in Exeter. I'm sure I could see to it that a place be found for —"

Mother interrupted, her fury only barely suppressed, her voice cold but still calm. "I could never do that, Colonel. Never. But if I want to keep a roof over our heads, then I have to find some way I can come to work for you as your wife's maid. That is what you're telling me, isn't it."

"I'd say you understand the position perfectly, Mrs. Peaceful. I couldn't have put it better myself. I shall need your agreement within the week. Good day, Mrs. Peaceful. And once again, my condolences."

We watched him go, leaving Mother standing there. I had never in my life seen her cry before, but she cried now. She fell on her knees in the long grass holding her face in her hands. That was when Big Joe and Molly came out of the cottage. When Big Joe saw Mother he ran and knelt down beside her, hugging and rocking her gently in his arms, singing *Oranges and Lemons* until she began to smile through her tears and join in. Then we were all singing together, and loudly in our defiance so that the Colonel could not help but hear us.

Later, after Molly had gone home, Charlie and I sat in silence in the orchard. I almost told him my secret then. I wanted to so badly. But I just couldn't bring myself to do it. I thought he might never speak to me again if I did. The moment passed. "I hate that man," said Charlie under his breath. "I'll do him, Tommo. One day I'll really do him."

Of course Mother had no choice. She had to take the job, and we only had one relative to turn to for help, Grandma Wolf. She moved in the next week to look after us. She wasn't our grandmother at all, not really — both our grandmothers were dead. She was Mother's aunt, but always insisted we called her "Grandma" because she thought Great Aunt made her sound old and crotchety, which she always was. We hadn't liked her before she moved in — as much on account of her mustache as anything else — and we liked her even less now that she had. We all knew her story; how she'd worked up at the Big House for the Colonel for years as housekeeper, and how, for some reason, the Colonel's wife couldn't stand her. They'd had a big falling out, and in the end she'd had to leave and go to live in the village. That was why she was free to come and look after us.

But between ourselves Charlie and I had never called her either Great Aunt or Grandma. We had our own name for her. When we were younger Mother had often read us *Little Red Riding Hood*. There was a picture in it Charlie and I knew well, of the wolf in bed pretending to be Little Red Riding Hood's grandma. She had a black bonnet on her head, like our "Grandma" always used to wear, and she had big teeth with gaps in between, just like our "Grandma" too. So ever since I could remember we had called her "Grandma Wolf" — never to her face, of course. Mother said it wasn't respectful, but secretly I think she always quite liked it.

Soon it wasn't only because of the book that we thought of her as Grandma Wolf. She very quickly showed us who was in charge now that Mother was not there. Everything had to be just so: hands washed, hair done, no talking with your mouth full, no leaving anything on your plate. "Waste not, want not," she'd say. That wasn't so bad. We got used to it. But what we could not forgive was that she was nasty to Big Joe. She talked to him, and about him, as if he were stupid or mad. She'd treat him as if he were a baby. She was forever wiping his mouth for him, or telling him not to sing at the table. When Molly protested once, she smacked her and sent her home. She smacked Big Joe too, whenever he didn't do what she said, which was often. He would start to rock then and talk to himself, which is what he always did whenever he was upset. But now Mother wasn't there to sing to him, to calm him. Molly talked to him, and we tried too, but it was not the same.

From the day Grandma Wolf moved in, our whole world changed. Mother would go to work up at the Big House at dawn, before we went off to school, and she still wouldn't be back when we got home for our tea. Instead Grandma Wolf would be there, at the door of what seemed to us now to be her lair. And Big Joe, who she wouldn't allow to go off on his wanders as he'd always loved to do, would come rushing up to us as if he hadn't seen us in weeks. He'd do the same to Mother when she came home, but she was often so exhausted she could hardly talk to him. She could see what was going on but was powerless to do anything about it. It seemed to all of us as if we were losing her, as if she was being replaced and pushed aside.

It was Grandma Wolf who did all the talking now, even telling Mother what to do in her own house. She was forever saying how Mother hadn't brought us up properly, that our manners were terrible, that we didn't know right from wrong — and that Mother had married beneath her. "I told her then and I've told her since," she ranted on, "she could have done far better for herself. But did she listen? Oh no. She had to marry the first man to turn her head, and him nothing but a forester. She was meant for better things, a better class of person. We were shopkeepers — we ran a proper shop, I can tell you — made a tidy profit too. In a big way of business, I'll have you know. But oh no, she wouldn't have it. Broke your grandfather's heart, she did. And now look what she's come to: a lady's maid, at her age. Trouble. Your mother's always been nothing but trouble from the day she was born."

We longed for Mother to stand up to her, but each time she just gave in meekly, too worn out to do anything else. To Charlie and me she seemed almost to have become a different person. There was no laughter in her voice, no light in her eyes. And all along I knew full well whose fault it was that this had all happened, that Father was dead, that Mother had to go to work up at the Big House, and that Grandma Wolf had moved in and taken her place.

At night we could sometimes hear Grandma Wolf snoring in bed, and Charlie and I would make up this story about the Colonel and Grandma Wolf; how one day we'd go up to the Big House and push the Colonel's wife into the lake and drown her, and then Mother could come home and be with us and Big Joe and Molly, and everything could be like it had been before. Then the Colonel and Grandma Wolf could marry one another and live unhappily ever after, and because they were so old they could have lots of little monster children born already old and wrinkly with gappy teeth: the girls with mustaches like Grandma Wolf, the boys with whiskers like the Colonel.

I remember I used to have nightmares filled with those monster children, but whatever my nightmare it would always end the same way. I would be out in the woods with Father and the tree would be falling, and I'd wake up screaming. Then Charlie would be there beside me, and everything would be all right again. Charlie always made things all right again.

NEARLY QUARTER PAST ELEVEN

There's a mouse in here with me. He's sitting there in the light of the lamp, looking up at me. He seems as surprised to see me as I am to see him. There he goes. I can hear him still, scurrying about somewhere under the hayrack. I think he's gone now. I hope he comes back. I miss him already.

❖   ❖   ❖

Grandma Wolf hated mice. She had a deep fear of them that she could not hide. So Charlie and I had lots to smile about in the autumn when the rain and the cold came and the mice decided it was warmer inside and came to live with us in the cottage. Big Joe loved the mice — he'd even put out food for them. Grandma Wolf would shout at him for that and smack him. But Big Joe could never understand why he was being smacked, so he went on feeding the mice just as he had before. Grandma Wolf put traps down, but Charlie and I would find them and spring them. All that autumn she only ever managed to catch one.

That mouse had the best funeral any mouse ever had. Big Joe was chief mourner and he cried enough for all of us. Molly, Charlie and I dug the grave, and when we'd laid him to rest Molly piled the grave high with flowers and sang *What a friend we have in Jesus*. We did all this at the bottom of the orchard hidden behind the apple trees where Grandma Wolf could not see or hear us. Afterwards we sat in a circle round the grave and had a funeral feast of blackberries. Big Joe stopped crying to eat the blackberries, and then with blackened mouths we all sang *Oranges and Lemons* over the mouse's grave.

Grandma Wolf tried everything to get rid of the mice. She put poison down under the sink in the larder. We swept it up. She asked Bob James, the wart charmer from the village with the crooked nose, to come and charm the mice away. He tried, but it didn't work. So in the end, in desperation, she had to resort to chasing them out of the house with a broom. But they just kept coming back in again. All this made her nastier than ever towards us. But for Charlie and me, just to see her frightened silly and screeching like a witch was worth every smack she gave us.

In bed at night our Grandma Wolf story was changing every time we told it. Now the Colonel and Grandma Wolf didn't have human children at all. Instead she gave birth to giant mice-children, all of them with great long tails and twitchy whiskers. But after what she did next, we decided that even that horrible fate was too good for her.

Although Grandma Wolf did smack Molly from time to time, it soon became obvious that she liked her a great deal better than the rest of us. There were good reasons for this. Girls were nice, Grandma Wolf would often tell us, not coarse and vulgar like boys. Besides, she was good friends with Molly's mother and father. They lived, as we did, in a cottage on the Colonel's estate — Molly's father was groom up at the Big House. They were *proper* people, Grandma Wolf told us; good, God-fearing people who had brought their child up well — which meant strictly. And from what Molly told us, they *were* strict too. She was forever being sent to her room, or strapped by her father for the least little thing. She was an only child of older parents and, as Molly often said, they wanted her to be perfect. Anyway, it was a good thing for us that Grandma approved of her family, otherwise I'm sure she would have forbidden Molly to come and see us. As it was, Grandma Wolf said Molly was a good influence, that she could teach us some manners, and make us a little less coarse and vulgar. So, thank goodness, Molly kept coming home with us for tea every day after school.

Not long after the mouse's funeral, it was Big Joe's birthday. Charlie and I had got him some humbugs from Mrs. Bright's shop in the village — which he always loved — and Molly brought him a present in a little brown box with air holes in it and elastic bands round it. While we were in school she kept it hidden in the shrubs at the bottom of the school yard. It was only because we pestered her that she showed us what it was as we were walking home. It was a harvest mouse, the sweetest little mouse I ever saw, with oversized ears and bewildered eyes. She stroked him with the back of her finger and he sat up for her in the box and twitched his whiskers at us. She gave him to Big Joe after tea, down in the orchard out of sight of the cottage, well hidden from Grandma Wolf's ever watchful gaze. Big Joe hugged Molly as if he'd never let her go. He kept the birthday mouse in his own box and hid him away in a drawer in his bedroom cupboard — he said it would be too cold for him outside in the woodshed with all his other creatures. The mouse became his instant favorite. All of us tried to make Big Joe understand that he mustn't ever tell Grandma Wolf, that if she ever knew, she'd take his mouse away and kill it.

I don't know how she found out, but when we came home from school a few days later Big Joe was sitting on the floor of his room, sobbing his heart out, his drawer empty beside him. Grandma Wolf came storming in saying she wasn't going to have any nasty dirty animals in *her* house. Worse still, so that he'd never bring any of his other animals into the house, she'd got rid of them all: the slowworm, the two lizards, the hedgehog. Big Joe's family of animals were gone, and he was heartbroken. Molly screamed at her that she was a cruel, cruel woman and that she'd go to Hell when she was dead, and then ran off home in tears.

That night Charlie and I made up a story about how we'd put rat poison in Grandma Wolf's tea the next day and kill her. We did get rid of her in the end too, but thankfully without the use of rat poison. Instead, a miracle happened, a wonderful miracle.

First, the Colonel's wife died in her wheelchair, so we didn't have to push her into the lake after all. She choked on a scone at teatime, and despite everything Mother did to try to save her, she just stopped breathing. There was a big funeral that we all had to go to. She had a shining coffin with silver handles, piled high with flowers. The vicar said how loved she was in the parish, and how she'd devoted her life to caring for everyone on the estate — all of which was news to us.

Afterwards they opened up the church floor and lowered her into the family vault while we all sang *Abide with me*. And I was thinking that I'd rather be in Father's simple coffin and buried outside where the sun shines and the wind blows, not down in some gloomy hole with a crowd of dead relatives. Mother had to take Big Joe out in the middle of the hymn because he started singing *Oranges and Lemons* again very loudly and would not stop. Grandma Wolf bared her teeth at us — as wolves do — and furrowed her brow in disapproval. We didn't know it then, but very soon she would disappear almost totally from our lives, taking all her anger, all her threats and disapproval with her.

So suddenly, joy of joys, Mother was back home with us again, and we hoped it was only a question of time before Grandma Wolf moved back up to the village. There was no job for Mother any more up at the Big House, no lady to be a maid to. She was home, and day by day she was becoming her old self again. There were wonderful blazing arguments between her and Grandma Wolf, mostly about how Grandma

Wolf treated Big Joe. Mother said that now that she was home she wouldn't stand for it any more. We listened to every word, and loved every moment of it. But there was one big shadow over all this new joy. We could see that with Mother out of work and no money coming in, things were becoming desperate. There was no money in the mug on the mantel-piece, and every day there was less food on the table. For a while we had little to eat but potatoes, and we all knew perfectly well that sooner or later the Colonel would put us out of the cottage. We were just waiting for the knock on the door. Meanwhile we were becoming very hungry.

It was Charlie's idea to go poaching: salmon, sea trout, rabbits, even deer if we were lucky, he said. Father had done a bit of poaching, so Charlie knew what to do. Molly and I would be on lookout. He could do the trapping or the fishing. So, at dusk, or dawn, whenever we could get away together, we went off poaching on the Colonel's land: in the Colonel's forests or in the Colonel's river where there were plenty of sea trout and plenty of salmon. We couldn't take Big Joe because he could start his singing at any time and give us away. Besides he'd tell Mother. He told Mother everything.

We did well. We brought back lots of rabbits, a few trout and, once, a fourteen-pound salmon. So now we had something to eat with our potatoes. We didn't tell Mother we'd been on to the Colonel's land. She wouldn't have approved of that sort of thing at all, and we definitely didn't want Grandma Wolf knowing because she'd certainly have gone and reported us to the Colonel at once. "My friend, the Colonel," she called him. She was always full of his praises, so we knew we had to be careful. We said we'd caught our rabbits in the orchard and the fish from the village brook. The trout you could catch there were only small, but they didn't know that. Charlie told them that the salmon must have come up the brook to spawn, which they did do, of course. Charlie always lied well, and they believed him. Thank God.

Molly and I would keep watch while Charlie set the traps or put out his nets. Lambert, the Colonel's bailiff, may have been old, but he was clever, and we knew he'd let his dog loose on us if he ever caught us at it. Late one evening, sitting by the bridge with Charlie busy at his nets downstream, Molly took my hand in hers and held it tight. "I don't like the dark," she whispered. I had never been so happy.

When the Colonel turned up at the house the next day, we thought it must be either because we'd been found out somehow or because he was going to evict us. It was neither. Grandma Wolf seemed to be expecting him, and that was strange. She went to the door and invited him in. He nodded at Mother and then frowned at us. Grandma Wolf waved us outside as she asked the Colonel to sit down. We tried eavesdropping but Big Joe was no good at keeping quiet, so we had to wait until later to hear the worst. As it turned out, the worst was not the worst at all, but the best.

After the Colonel had gone, Grandma Wolf called us in. I could see she was puffed up with self-importance, aglow with it. "Your mother will explain," she declared grandly, putting on her bonnet. "I have to get up to the Big House right away. I've work to do."

Mother waited until she'd gone and could not help smiling as she told us. "Well," she began, "you know some time ago your great aunt used to work as housekeeper up at the Big House?"

"And then she got kicked out by the Colonel's wife," said Charlie.

"She lost her job, yes," Mother went on. "Well, now the Colonel's wife has passed away it seems the Colonel wants her back as live-in housekeeper. She'll be moving up to the Big House as soon as possible."

I didn't cheer, but I certainly felt like it.

"What about the cottage?" Charlie asked. "Is the old duffer putting us out then?"

"No, dear. We're staying put," Mother replied. "He said his wife had liked me and made him promise to look after me if ever anything happened to her. So he's keeping that promise. Say what you like about the Colonel, he's a man of his word. I've agreed I'll do all his linen for him and his sewing work. Most of it I can bring home. So we'll have some money coming in. We'll manage. Well, are you happy? We're staying put!"

Then we did cheer and Big Joe cheered too, louder than any of us. So we stayed on in our cottage and Grandma Wolf moved out. We were liberated, and all was right with the world again. For a while at least.

Both of them being older than me, Molly by two years, Charlie by three, they always ran faster than I did. I seem to have spent much of my life watching them racing ahead of me, leaping the high meadow grass, Molly's plaits whirling about her head, their laughter mingling. When they got too far ahead I sometimes felt they wanted to be without me. I would whine at them then to let them know I was feeling all miserable and abandoned, and they'd wait for me to catch up. Best of all Molly would sometimes come running back and take my hand.

When we weren't poaching the Colonel's fish or scrumping his apples — more than anything we all loved the danger of it I think — we would be roaming wild in the countryside. Molly could shin up a tree like a cat, faster than either of us. Sometimes we'd go down to the river bank and watch the kingfishers flash by, or we'd go swimming in Okement Pool hung all around by willows, where the water was dark and deep and mysterious, and where no one ever came.

I remember the day Molly dared Charlie to take off all his clothes, and to my amazement he did. Then she did, and they ran shrieking and bare-bottomed into the water. When they called me in after them, I wouldn't do it, not in front of Molly. So I sat and sulked on the bank and watched them splashing and giggling, and all the while I was wishing I had the courage to do what Charlie had done, wishing I was with them. Molly got dressed afterwards behind a bush and told us not to watch. But we did. That was the first time I ever saw a girl with no clothes on. She was very thin and white, and she wrung her plaits out like a wet cloth.

It was several days before they managed to entice me in. Molly stood waist-deep in the river and put her hands over her eyes. "Come on, Tommo," she cried. "I won't watch. Promise." And not wanting to be left out yet again, I stripped off and made a dash for the river, covering myself as I went just in case Molly was watching through her fingers. After I'd done it that first time, it never seemed to bother me again.

Sometimes when we tired of all the frolicking we'd lie and talk in the shallows, letting the river ripple over us. How we talked. Molly told us once that she wanted to die right there and then, that she never wanted tomorrow to come because no tomorrow could ever be as good as today. "I know," she said, and she sat up in the river then and collected a handful of small pebbles. "I'm going to tell our future. I've seen the gypsies do it." She shook the pebbles around in her cupped hands, closed her eyes and then scattered them out on to the muddy shore. Kneeling over them she spoke very seriously and slowly, as if she were reading them. "They say we'll always be together, the three of us, for ever and ever. They say that as long as we stick together we'll be lucky and happy." Then she smiled at us. "And the stones never lie," she said. "So you're stuck with me."

For a year or two Molly's stones proved right. But then Molly got ill. She wasn't at school one day. It was the scarlet fever, Mr. Munnings told us, and very serious. Charlie and I went up to her cottage that evening after tea with some sweetpeas Mother had picked for her — because they smell sweeter than any flower she knew, she said. We knew we wouldn't be allowed in to see her because scarlet fever was very catching, but Molly's mother did not look at all pleased to see us. She always looked grey and grim, but that day she was angry as well. She took the flowers with scarcely a glance at them, and told us it would be better if we didn't come again. Then Molly's father appeared from behind her, looking gruff and unkempt, and told us to be off, that we were disturbing Molly's sleep. As I walked away, all I could think of was how unhappy Molly must be living in that dingy little cottage with a mother and father like that, and how trees fall on the wrong fathers. We stopped at the end of the path and looked up at Molly's window, hoping she would come and wave at us. When she didn't we knew she must be really ill.

Charlie and I never said our prayers at all any more, not since Sunday school, but we did now. Kneeling side by side with Big Joe we prayed each night that Molly would not die. Joe sang *Oranges and Lemons* and we said *Amen* afterwards. We had our fingers crossed too, just for good measure.

TEN TO MIDNIGHT

I'm not sure I ever really believed in God, even in Sunday school. In church I'd gaze up at Jesus hanging on the cross in the stained-glass window, and feel sorry for him because I could see how cruel it was and how much it must be hurting him. I knew he was a good and kind man. But I never really understood why God, who was supposed to be his father, and almighty and powerful, would let them do that to him, would let him suffer so much. I believed then, as I believe now, that crossed fingers and Molly's stones are every bit as reliable or unreliable as praying to God. I shouldn't think like that because if there's no God, then there can be no heaven. Tonight I want very much to believe there's a heaven, that, as Father said, there is a new life after death, that death is not a full stop, and that we will all see one another again.

❖   ❖   ❖

It was while Molly was ill in bed with the scarlet fever that Charlie and I discovered that although in one way Molly's stones had let us down, in another way they had indeed spoken the truth: with her, with the three of us together, we *were* lucky, and without her we weren't. Up until now, whenever the three of us had gone out together poaching the Colonel's fish, we had never been caught. We'd had a few close shaves with old Lambert and his dog, but our lookout system had always worked. Somehow we'd always heard them coming and managed to make ourselves scarce. But the very first time Charlie and I went out poaching without Molly, things went wrong, badly wrong, and it was my fault.

We had chosen a perfect poaching night; not a breath of wind, so we could hear anyone coming. With Molly beside me on lookout I'd never felt sleepy, and we'd always heard old Lambert and his dog in plenty of time for Charlie to get out of the river, for us all to make good our escape. But on this particular night my concentration failed me. I'd made myself comfortable, probably too comfortable, in our usual place by the bridge with Charlie netting downstream. But after sitting there for a while I just fell asleep. I don't drop off all that easily, but when I do sleep I sleep deeply.

The first I knew of anything was a dog snuffling at my neck. Then he was barking in my face, and old Lambert was dragging me to my feet. And there was Charlie way out in the middle of the moonlit river hauling at the nets.

"Peaceful boys! You young rascals," Lambert growled. "Caught you red-handed. You're in for it now, make no mistake."

Charlie could have left me there. He could have made a run for it and got clean away, but Charlie's not like that. He never has been.

At the point of a shotgun Lambert marched us back along the river and up to the Big House, his dog snarling at our heels from time to time just to remind us he was still there, and that he'd eat us alive if we made a run for it. Lambert locked us in the stables and left us. We waited in the darkness, the horses shifting and munching and snorting around us. All too soon we saw the approaching light of a lamp, and heard footsteps and voices. Then the Colonel was there in his slippers and his dressing gown, and he had Grandma Wolf with him in her nightcap, looking every bit as fierce as Lambert's dog.

The Colonel looked from one to the other of us, shaking his head in disgust. But Grandma Wolf had the first word. "I've never in all my life been so ashamed," she said. "My own family. You're nothing but a downright disgrace. And after all the Colonel's done for us. Common thieves, that's what you are. Nothing but common thieves."

When she'd finished it was the Colonel's turn. "Only one way to deal with young ruffians like you," he said. "I could have you up before the magistrate, but since I'm the magistrate anyway there's no need to go to all that trouble, is there? I'll sentence you right now. You will come up here tomorrow morning at ten o'clock sharp, and I'll give each of you the hiding you so richly deserve. Then you can stay and clean out the hunt kennels till I say you can go. That should teach you not to come poaching on my land."

When we got home we had to tell Mother everything we'd done, everything the Colonel had said. Charlie did most of the talking. Mother sat listening in silence, her face stony. When she spoke, she spoke in little more than a whisper. "I can tell you one thing," she said. "There'll be no hiding. Over my dead body." Then she looked up at us, her eyes full of tears. "Why? You said you'd been fishing in the brook. You told me. Oh Charlie, Tommo." Big Joe stroked her hair. He was anxious and bewildered. She patted his arm. "It's all right, Joe. I'll go up there with them tomorrow. Cleaning out the kennels I don't mind — you deserve that. But it stops there. I won't let that man lay a finger on you, not one finger, no matter what."

Mother was as good as her word. How she did it and what was said we never knew, but the next day after Mother and the Colonel had had a meeting in his study, she made us stand in front of him and apologize. Then after a long lecture about trespassing on private property, the Colonel said that he'd changed his mind, that instead of the hiding we would be set to cleaning out the Colonel's kennels every Saturday and Sunday until Christmas.

As it turned out we didn't mind at all because, although the smell could be disgusting, the hounds were all around us as we worked, their tails high and waving and happy. So we often stopped work to pet them, after we'd made quite sure no one was looking. We had a particular favorite called Bertha. She was almost pure white with one brown foot and had the most beautiful eyes. She would always stand near us as we scraped and swept, gazing up at us in open adoration. Every time I looked into her eyes I thought of Molly. Like Bertha, she too had eyes the color of heather honey.

We had to be careful, because Grandma Wolf, now more full of herself than ever, would frequently come out into the stable yard to make sure we were doing our work properly. She'd always have something nasty to say: "Serves you right," or "That'll teach you," or "You should be ashamed of yourselves," always delivered with a tut and a pained sigh. To finish there'd be some nasty quip about Mother. "Still, with a mother like that, I suppose you're not entirely to blame, are you?"

Then Christmas Eve came and our punishment was over at last. We said fond farewells to Bertha and ran off home down the Colonel's drive for the last time, blowing very loud raspberries as we went. Back in the cottage we found waiting for us the best Christmas present we could ever have hoped for. Molly was sitting there smiling at us as we came in through the door. She was pale, but she was back with us. We were together again. Her hair was cut shorter. The plaits were gone, and somehow that changed the whole look of her. She wasn't a girl any more. She had a different beauty now, a beauty that at once stirred in me a new and deeper love.

I think, without knowing it, I had always charted my own growing up by constant comparison to Molly and Charlie. Day by day I was becoming ever more painfully aware of how far behind them I was. I wasn't just smaller and slower than they were — I had never liked that, but I was used to it by now. The trouble was that it was becoming evident to me that the gap between us was more serious, and that it was widening. It really began when Molly was moved up into the Bigguns' class. I was stuck being a Tiddler and they were growing away from me. But whilst we were still at the village school together I didn't mind all that much because at least I was always near them. We walked to school together, ate our lunch together as we always had — up in the pantry in the vicarage, where the vicar's wife would bring us lemonade — and then we'd come home together.

I looked forward all day to that long walk home, the school day done, their other friends not with us, with the fearsome Mr. Munnings out of sight and out of mind for another day. We'd hare down the hill to the brook, pull off our great heavy boots and release our aching feet and toes at long last. We'd sit there on the bank wiggling our toes in the blessed cool of the water. We'd lie amongst the grass and buttercups of the water meadows and look up at the clouds scudding across the sky, at the wind-whipped crows chasing a mewing buzzard. Then we'd follow the brook home, feet squelching in the mud, our toes oozing with it. Strange when I think of it now, but there was a time when I loved mud, the smell of it, the feel of it, the larking about in it. Not any more.

Then quite suddenly, just after my twelfth birthday, the last of the larking was all over. Charlie and Molly left school and I was alone. I was a Biggun, in Mr. Munnings' class and hating him now even more than I feared him. I woke up dreading every day. Both Charlie and Molly had found work up in the Big House — almost everyone in the village worked up there or on the estate. Molly was under-parlor maid, and Charlie worked in the hunt kennels and in the stables looking after the dogs and the horses, which he loved. Molly didn't come round to see us nearly so often as before — like Charlie, she worked six days a week. So I hardly saw her.

Charlie would come home late in the evenings as Father had before him, and he'd hang his coat up on Father's peg and put his boots outside on the porch where Father's boots had always been. He warmed his feet in the bottom oven when he came in out of the cold of a winter's day, just as Father had done. That was the first time in my life I was ever really jealous of Charlie. I wanted to put *my* feet in the oven, and to come home from proper work, to earn money like Charlie did, to have a voice that didn't pipe like the little children in Miss McAllister's class. Most of all though I wanted to be with Molly again. I wanted us to be a threesome again, for everything to be just as it had been. But nothing stays the same. I learnt that then. I know that now.

At nights as Charlie and I lay in bed together Charlie just slept. We never made up our stories any more. When I did see Molly, and it was only on Sundays now, she was as kind to me as she always had been, but too kind almost, too protective, more like a little mother to me than a friend. I could see that she and Charlie lived in another world now. They talked endlessly about the goings on and scandals up at the Big House, about the prowling Wolfwoman — it was around this time they dropped the "Grandma" altogether and began to call her "Wolfwoman." That was when I first heard the gossip about the Colonel and the Wolfwoman. Charlie said they'd had a thing going for years — common knowledge. That was why the late "Mrs. Colonel" had kicked her out all those years before. And now they were like husband and wife up there, only she wore the trousers. There was talk of the Colonel's dark moods, how he'd shut himself up in his study all day sometimes, and of Cook's tantrums whenever things were not done just so. It was a world I could not be part of, a world I did not belong in.

I tried all I could to interest them in my life at school. I told them about how we'd all heard Miss McAllister and Mr. Munnings having a blazing argument because he refused to light the school stove, how she'd called him a wicked, wicked man. She was right too. Mr. Munnings would never light the stove unless the puddles were iced over in the school yard, unless our fingers were so cold we couldn't write. He shouted back at her that he would light the stove when he thought fit, and that anyway suffering was part of life and good for a child's soul. Charlie and Molly made out that they were interested, but I could tell they weren't. Then one day down by the brook, I turned and saw them walking away from me through the water meadows holding hands. We'd all held hands before, often, but then it had been the three of us. I knew at once that this was different. As I watched them I felt a sudden ache in my heart. I don't think it was anger or jealousy, more a pang of loss, of deep grief.

We did have some moments when we became a threesome again, but they were becoming all too few and far between. I remember the day of the yellow airplane. It was the first airplane any of us had ever seen. We'd heard about them, seen pictures of them, but until that day I don't think I ever really believed they were real, that they actually flew. You had to see one to believe it. Molly and Charlie and I were fishing down in the brook, just for tiddlers, or brown trout if we were lucky — we'd done no more salmon poaching, Mother had made us promise.

It was late on a summer evening and we were just about to set off home when we heard the distant sound of an engine. At first we thought it was the Colonel's car — his Rolls Royce was the only car for miles around — but then we all realized at the same moment that this was a different kind of engine altogether. It was a sound of intermittent droning, like a thousand stuttering bees. What's more, it wasn't coming from the road at all; it was coming from high above us. There was a flurry of squawking and splashing further upstream as a flight of ducks took off in a panic. We ran out from under the trees to get a better look. An airplane! We watched, spellbound, as it circled above us like some ungainly yellow bird, its great wide wings wobbling precariously. We could see the goggled pilot looking down at us out of the cockpit. We waved frantically up at him and he waved back. Then he was coming in lower, lower. The cows in the water meadow scattered. The airplane was coming in to land, bouncing, then bumping along and coming to a stop some fifty yards away from us.

The pilot didn't get out, but beckoned us over. We didn't hesitate. "Better not switch off!" he shouted over the roar of the engine. He was laughing as he lifted up his goggles. "Might never get the damn thing started again. Listen, the truth is I reckon I'm a bit lost. That church up there on the hill, is that Lapford church?"

"No," Charlie shouted back. "That's Iddesleigh. St. James."

The pilot looked down at his map. "Iddesleigh? You sure?"

"Yes," we shouted.

"Whoops! Then I really was lost. Jolly good thing I

stopped, wasn't it? Thanks for your help. Better be off." He lowered his goggles and smiled at us. "Here. You like humbugs?" And he reached out and handed Charlie a bag of sweets. "Cheerio then," he said. "Stand well back. Here we go."

And with that, off he went bouncing along towards the hedge, his engine spluttering. I thought he couldn't possibly lift off in time. He managed it, but only just, his wheels clipping the top of the hedge, before he was up and away. He did one steep turn, then flew straight at us. There was no time to run. All we could do was throw ourselves face down in the long grass. We felt the sudden blast of the wind as he passed above us. By the time we rolled over he was climbing up over the trees and away. We could see him laughing and waving. We watched him soaring over Iddesleigh church tower and then away into the distance. He was gone, leaving us lying there breathless in the silence he'd left behind.

For some time afterwards we lay there in the long grass watching a single skylark rising above us, and sucking on our humbugs. When Charlie came to share them out we had five each, and five for Big Joe too.

"Was that real?" Molly breathed. "Did it really happen?"

"We've got our humbugs," said Charlie, "so it must have been real, mustn't it?"

"Every time I eat humbugs from now on," Molly said,

"every time I look at skylarks, I'm going to think of that yellow airplane, and the three of us, and how we are right now."

"Me too," I said.

"Me too," said Charlie.

Most people in the village had seen the airplane, but only we three had been there when it landed, only we had talked to the pilot. I was so proud of that — too proud as it turned out. I told the story, several embellished versions of it, again and again at school, showing everyone my humbugs just to prove all I'd said was true. But someone must have snitched on me, because Mr. Munnings came straight over to me in class and, for no reason at all, told me to empty out my pockets. I had three of my precious humbugs left and he confiscated them all. Then he took me by the ear to the front of the class where he gave me six strokes of the ruler in his own very special way, sharp edge down on to my knuckles. As he did it I looked him in the eye and stared him out. It didn't dull the pain, nor I'm sure did it make him feel bad about what he was doing, but my sullen defiance of him made me feel a lot better as I walked back to my desk.

As I lay in bed that night, my knuckles still throbbing, I was longing to tell Charlie about what had happened at school, but I knew that everything about school bored him now, so I said nothing. But the longer I lay there thinking about my knuckles and my humbugs the more I was bursting to talk to him. I could hear from his breathing that he was still awake. For just a moment it occurred to me this might be the time to tell him about Father, and how I'd killed him in the forest all those years before. That at least would interest him. I did try, but I still could not summon up the courage to tell him. In the end all I told him was that Mr. Munnings had confiscated my humbugs. "I hate him," I said. "I hope he chokes on them." Even as I was speaking I could tell he wasn't listening.

"Tommo," he whispered, "I'm in trouble."

"What've you done?" I asked him.

"I'm in real trouble, but I had to do it. You remember Bertha, that whitey-looking foxhound up at the Big House, the one we liked?"

"Course," I said.

"Well, she's always been my favorite ever since. And then this afternoon the Colonel comes by the kennels and tells me . . . he tells me he's going to have to shoot Bertha. So I ask him why. Because she's getting a bit old, a bit slow, he says. Because whenever they go out hunting she's always going off on her own and getting herself lost. She's no use for hunting any more, he says, no use to anyone. I asked him not to, Tommo. I told him she was my favorite. 'Favorite!' he says, laughing at

57

me. 'Favorite? How can you have a favorite? Lot of sentimental claptrap. She's just one of a pack of dumb beasts, boy, and don't you forget it!' I begged him, Tommo. I told him he shouldn't do it. That's when he got really angry. He said they're his foxhounds and he'd shoot them as and when he felt like it, and he didn't want any more lip from me about it. So you know what I did, Tommo? I stole her. I ran off with her after dark, through the trees so no one would see us."

"Where is she now?" I asked. "What've you done with her?"

"Remember that old forester's shack Father used, up in Ford's Cleave Wood? I've put her in there for the night. I gave her some food. Molly pinched some meat for me from the kitchen. She'll be all right up there. No one'll hear her, with a bit of luck anyway."

"But what'll you do with her tomorrow? What if the Colonel finds out?"

"I don't know, Tommo," Charlie said. "I don't know."

We hardly slept a wink that night. I lay there listening out for Bertha all the while. When I did drop off, I kept waking up suddenly, thinking I had heard Bertha barking. But always it turned out to be a screeching fox. And once it was an owl hooting, right outside our window.

TWENTY-FOUR MINUTES PAST TWELVE

I haven't seen a fox while I've been out here. It's hardly surprising, I suppose. But I have heard owls. How any bird can survive in all this I'll never know. I've even seen larks over no-man's-land. I always found hope in that.

❖   ❖   ❖

"He'll know," Charlie whispered to me in bed at dawn. "As soon as they find Bertha gone, the Colonel will know it was me. I won't tell him where she is. I don't care what he does, I won't tell him."

Charlie and I ate our breakfast in silence, hoping the inevitable storm wouldn't break, but knowing that sooner or later it must. Big Joe sensed something was wrong — he could always feel anxiety in the air. He was rocking back and forth and wouldn't touch his breakfast. So then Mother knew something was up as well. Once she was suspicious Mother was a difficult person to hide things from, and we weren't very good at it, not that morning.

"Is Molly coming over?" she asked, beginning to probe.

There was a loud and insistent knocking on the door. She could tell at once it wouldn't be Molly. It was too early for Molly, and anyway she didn't knock like that. Besides, I think she could already see from our faces that Charlie and I were expecting an unwelcome visitor. As we feared, it was the Colonel.

Mother invited him in. He stood there glaring at us, thin-lipped and pale with fury. "I think you know why I've come, Mrs. Peaceful," he began.

"No, Colonel, I don't," said Mother.

"So the young devil hasn't told you." He was shouting now, shaking his stick at Charlie. Big Joe began to whimper and clutched Mother's hand as the Colonel ranted on.

"That boy of yours is a despicable thief. First of all he steals the salmon out of my river. And now, in my employ, in a position of trust, he steals one of my foxhounds. Don't deny it, boy. I know it was you. Where is she? Is she here? Is she?"

Mother looked to Charlie for an explanation.

"He was going to shoot her, Mother," he said quickly. "I had to do it."

"You see!" roared the Colonel. "He admits it! He admits it!"

Big Joe was beginning to wail now and Mother was smoothing his hair, trying to reassure and comfort him as she spoke. "So you took her in order to save her, Charlie, is that right?"

"Yes, Mother."

"Well, you shouldn't have done that, Charlie, should you?"

"No, Mother."

"Will you tell the Colonel where you've hidden her?"

"No, Mother."

Mother thought for a moment or two. "I didn't think so," she said. She looked the Colonel full in the face. "Colonel, am I right in thinking that if you were going to shoot this dog, presumably it was because she's no use to you any more — as a foxhound I mean?"

"Yes," the Colonel replied, "but what I do with my own animals, or why I do it, is no business of yours, Mrs. Peaceful. I don't have to explain myself to you."

"Of course not, Colonel," Mother spoke softly, sweetly

almost, "but if you were going to shoot her anyway, then you wouldn't mind if I were to take her off your hands and look after her, would you?"

"You can do what you like with the damned dog," the Colonel snapped. "You can bloody well eat her for all I care. But your son stole her from me and I will not let that go unpunished."

Mother asked Big Joe to fetch the money mug from the mantelpiece. "Here, Colonel," she said, calmly offering him a coin from the money mug. "Sixpence. I'm buying the dog off you for sixpence, not a bad price for a useless dog. So now it's not stolen, is it?"

The Colonel was utterly dumbfounded. He looked from the coin in his hand to Mother, to Charlie. He was breathing hard. Then, regaining his composure, he pocketed the sixpence in his waistcoat and pointed his stick at Charlie. "Very well, but you can consider yourself no longer in my employ." With that he turned on his heel and went out, slamming the door behind him. We listened to his footsteps going down the path, heard the front gate squeaking.

Charlie and I went mad, mostly out of sheer relief, but also quite overwhelmed with gratitude and admiration. What a mother we had! We whooped and yahooed. Big Joe was happy again, and sang *Oranges and Lemons* as he gambolled wildly round the kitchen.

"I don't know what you've got to be so almightily pleased about," said Mother when we had all calmed down. "You do know you've just lost your job, Charlie?"

"I don't care," said Charlie. "He can stuff his stinking job. I'll find another. You put the silly old fart in his place good and proper. And we've got Bertha."

"Where is that dog anyway?" Mother asked.

"I'll show you," Charlie said.

We waited for Molly to come and then we all went off up to Ford's Cleave Wood together. As we neared the shack, we could hear Bertha yowling. Charlie ran on ahead and opened the door. Out she came, bounding up to us, squeaking with delight, her tail swiping at our legs. She jumped up at all of us, licking everything she could, but right away she seemed to attach herself particularly to Big Joe. She followed him everywhere after that. She even slept on his bed at nights — Big Joe insisted on that no matter how much Mother protested. She'd sit under his apple tree howling up at him while he sang to her from high up in the branches. He only had to start singing and she'd join in, so from now on he never sang his *Oranges and Lemons* unaccompanied. He never did anything unaccompanied. They were always together. He fed her, brushed her and cleared up her frequent puddles (which were more like lakes). Big Joe had found a new friend and he was in seventh heaven.

After a few weeks going round all the farms in the parish looking for work, Charlie found a job as dairyman and shepherd at Farmer Cox's place on the other side of the village. He would go off before dawn on his bicycle to do the milking and was back home late, so I saw even less of him than before. He should have been much happier up there. He liked the cows and the sheep, though he said that the sheep were a bit stupid. Best of all, he said, he didn't have the Colonel or the Wolfwoman breathing down his neck all day.

But Charlie, like me, was very far from happy, because Molly had suddenly stopped coming. Mother said she was sure there could only be one reason. Someone must have put it about — and she thought it could only be the Colonel or the Wolfwoman or both — that Charlie Peaceful was a thieving rascal, and that therefore the Peaceful family were no longer considered fit folk for Molly to visit. She said Charlie should just let things cool down for a while, that Molly would be back. But Charlie wouldn't listen. Time after time he went to Molly's cottage. They wouldn't even answer the door. In the end, because he thought I'd have a better chance of getting to see Molly, he sent me over with a letter. Somehow, he said, I had to deliver it to her. I had to.

Molly's mother met me at the door with a face like thunder. "Go away," she yelled at me. "Just go away. Don't you understand? We don't want your kind here. We don't want you bothering our Molly. She doesn't want to see you." And with that she slammed the door in my face. I was walking away, Charlie's letter still in my pocket, when I happened to glance back and saw Molly waving at me frantically through her window. She was mouthing something I couldn't understand at all at first, gesticulating at me, pointing down the hill towards the brook. I knew then exactly what she meant me to do.

I ran down to the brook and waited under the trees where we'd always done our fishing together. I didn't have long to wait before she came. She took my hand without a word, and led me down under the bank where we couldn't possibly be seen. She was crying as she told me everything: how the Colonel had come to the cottage — she'd overheard it all — how he'd told her father that Charlie Peaceful was a thief; how he'd heard Charlie Peaceful had been seeing much more of Molly than was good for her, and that if he had any sense Molly's father should put a stop to it. "So my father won't let me see Charlie any more. He won't let me see any of you," Molly told me, brushing away her tears. "I'm so miserable without you, Tommo. I hate it up at the Big House without Charlie, and I hate it at home too. Father'll strap me if I see Charlie. And he said he'll take a gun to Charlie if he ever comes near me. I think he means it too."

"Why?" I asked. "Why's he like that?"

"He's always been like that," she said. "He says I'm wicked. Born in sin. Mother says he's only trying to save me from myself, so I won't go to Hell. He's always talking about Hell. I won't go to Hell, will I, Tommo?"

I did what I did next without thinking. I leant over and kissed her on the cheek. She threw her arms around my neck, sobbing as if her heart would break. "I so want to see Charlie," she cried. "I miss him so much." That was when I remembered to give her the letter. She tore it open and read it at once. It can't have been long because she read it so quickly. "Tell him yes. Yes, I will," she said, her eyes suddenly bright again.

"Just yes?" I asked, intrigued, puzzled and jealous all at the same time.

"Yes. Same time, same place, tomorrow. I'll write a letter back and you can give it to Charlie. All right?" She got up and pulled me to my feet. "I love you, Tommo. I love you both. And Big Joe, and Bertha." She kissed me quickly and was gone.

That was the first of dozens of letters I delivered from

Charlie to Molly and from Molly to Charlie over the weeks and months that followed. All through my last year at school I was their go-between postman. I didn't mind that much, because it meant I got to see Molly often, which was all that really mattered to me. It was all done in great secrecy — Charlie insisted on that. He made me swear on the Holy Bible to tell no one, not even Mother. He made me cross my heart and hope to die.

Molly and I would meet most evenings and exchange letters in the same place, down by the brook, both of us having made quite sure we were not followed. We'd sit and talk there for a few precious minutes, often with the rain dripping through the trees, and once I remember with the wind roaring about us so violently that I thought the trees might come down on us. Fearing for our lives, we ran out across the meadow and burrowed our way into the bottom of a haystack and sat there shivering like a couple of frightened rabbits.

It was in the shelter of this haystack that I first heard news of the war. When Molly talked it was often, if not always, about Charlie — she'd forever be asking news of him. I never showed her I minded, but I did. So I was quite pleased that day when she started telling me about how all the talk up at the Big House these days was of war with Germany, how everyone now thought it would happen sooner rather than later. She'd read about it herself in the newspaper, so she knew it had to be true.

It was Molly's job every morning, she told me, to iron the Colonel's *Times* newspaper before she took it to him in his study. Apparently he insisted his newspaper should be crisp and dry, so that the ink should not come off on his fingers while he was reading it. She didn't really understand what the war was all about, she admitted, only that some archduke — whatever that was — had been shot in a place called Sarajevo — wherever that was — and Germany and France were very angry with each other about it. They were gathering their armies to fight with each other and, if they did, then we'd be in it soon because we'd have to fight on the French side against the Germans. She didn't know why. It made about as much sense to me as it did to her. She said the Colonel was in a terrible mood about it all, and that everyone up at the Big House was much more frightened of his moods than they were about the war.

But apparently the Colonel was gentle as a lamb compared to the Wolfwoman these days (everyone called her that now, not just us). It seemed that someone had put salt in her tea instead of sugar and she swore it was on purpose — which it probably was, Molly said. She'd been ranting and raving about it ever since, telling everyone how she'd find out who it was. Meanwhile she was treating all of them as if they were guilty.

"Was it you?" I asked Molly.

"Maybe," she said, smiling, "and maybe not." I wanted to kiss her again then, but I didn't dare. That has always been my trouble. I've never dared enough.

Mother had it all arranged before I left school. I was to go and work with Charlie up at Mr. Cox's farm. Farmer Cox was getting on in years and, with no sons of his own, was in need of more help on the farm. He was a bit keen on the drink too, Charlie said. It was true. He was in the pub most evenings. He liked his beer and his skittles, and he liked to sing too. He knew all the old songs. He kept them in his head, but he'd only sing if he'd had a couple of beers. So he never sang on the farm. He was always rather dour on the farm, but fair, always fair.

I went up there mostly to look after the horses at first. For me it couldn't have been better. I was with Charlie again, working alongside him on the farm. I'd put on a spurt and was almost as tall as him by now, but still not as fast, nor as strong. He was a bit bossy with me sometimes, but that didn't bother me — that was his job after all. Things were changing between us. Charlie didn't treat me like a boy any more, and I liked that, I liked that a lot.

The newspapers were full of the war that had now begun, but aside from the army coming to the village and buying up lots of the local farm horses for cavalry horses, it had hardly touched us at all. Not yet. I was still Charlie's postman, still Molly's postman. So I saw Molly often, though not as often as before. For some reason the letters between them seemed less frequent. But at least with me now working with Charlie for six days a week we were all three together again in a kind of way, linked by the letters. Then that link was cruelly broken, and what followed broke my heart, broke all our hearts.

I remember Charlie and I had been haymaking with Farmer Cox, young buzzards wheeling above us all day, swallows skimming the mown grass all about us as the shadows lengthened and the evening darkened. We arrived home later than usual, dusty and exhausted, and hungry too. Inside we found Mother sitting upright in her chair doing her sewing, and opposite her Molly and, to our surprise, her mother. Everyone in the room looked as grim-faced as Molly's mother, even Big Joe, even Molly, whose eyes I could see were red from crying. Bertha was howling ominously from outside in the woodshed.

70

"Charlie," said Mother, setting her sewing aside. "Molly's mother has been waiting for you. She has something she wants to say to you."

"Yours, I believe," said Molly's mother, her voice as hard as stone. She handed Charlie a packet of letters tied up with a blue ribbon. "I found them. I've read them, every one of them. So has Molly's father. So we know, we know everything. Don't bother to deny it, Charlie Peaceful. The evidence is here, in these letters. Molly has been punished already, her father has seen to that. I've never read anything so wicked in all my life. Never. All that love talk. Disgusting. But you've been meeting as well, haven't you?"

Charlie looked across at Molly. The look between them said it all, and I knew then that I had been betrayed.

"Yes," said Charlie.

I couldn't believe what he was saying. They hadn't told me. They'd been meeting in secret and neither of them had told me.

"There. Didn't I tell you, Mrs. Peaceful?" Molly's mother went on, her voice quivering with rage.

"I'm sorry," said Mother. "But you'll still have to tell me why it is they shouldn't be meeting. Charlie's seventeen now, and Molly sixteen. Old enough, I'd say. I'm sure we both had our little rendezvous here and there when we were their age."

"You speak for yourself, Mrs. Peaceful," Molly's mother replied with a supercilious sneer. "Molly's father and I made it quite plain to both of them. We forbade them to have anything to do with each other. It's wickedness, Mrs. Peaceful, pure wickedness. The Colonel has warned us, you know, about your son's wicked thieving ways. Oh yes, we know all about him."

"Really?" said Mother. "Tell me, do you always do what the Colonel says? Do you always think what the Colonel thinks? If he said the earth was flat, would you believe him? Or did he just threaten you? He's good at that."

Molly's mother stood up, full of righteous indignation. "I haven't come here to argue the toss. I have come to tell of your son's misdemeanors, to say that I won't have him leading our Molly into the ways of wickedness and sin. He must never see her again, do you hear? If he does, then the Colonel will know about it. I'm telling you the Colonel will know about it. I have no more to say. Come along, Molly." And taking Molly's hand firmly in hers she swept out, leaving us all looking at one another and listening to Bertha still howling.

"Well," said Mother after a while. "I'll get your supper, boys, shall I?"

That night I lay there beside Charlie not speaking. I was so filled with anger and resentment towards him that I never wanted to speak to him again, nor to Molly, come to that. Then out of our silence he said: "All right, I should've told you, Tommo. Molly said I should tell you. But I didn't want to. I couldn't, that's all."

"Why not?" I asked. For several moments he did not reply.

"Because I know, and she does too. That's why she wouldn't tell you herself," Charlie said.

"Know what?"

"When it was just letters, it didn't seem to matter so much. But later, after we began seeing each other . . . we didn't want to hide it from you, Tommo, honest. But we didn't want to hurt you either. You love her, don't you?" I didn't answer. There was no need. "Well, so do I, Tommo. So you'll understand why I'm going to go on seeing her. I'll find a way no matter what that old cow says." He turned to me. "Still friends?" he said.

"Friends," I mumbled, but I did not mean it.

After that no more was ever said between us about Molly. I never asked because I didn't want to know. I didn't want even to think about it, but I did. I thought about nothing else.

No one could understand why, but shortly after this Bertha began to go missing from time to time. She hadn't wandered off at all until now; she'd always stuck close to Big Joe. Wherever Big Joe was, that's where you'd be sure to find

Bertha. Big Joe was frantic with worry every time she went off. She'd come back home in the end, of course, when she felt like it, either that or Mother and Joe would find her somewhere all muddied and wet and lost, and they'd bring her home. But the great worry was that she'd start chasing after sheep or cows, that some farmer or landowner would shoot her, as they'd shoot any dog they found trespassing on their land that could be molesting their animals. Fortunately Bertha didn't seem to go chasing sheep, and anyway up until now she had never been gone that long, nor strayed too far.

We did our very best to keep her from wandering. Mother tried shutting her in the woodshed, but Big Joe couldn't stand her howling and would let her out. She tried tying her up, but Bertha would chew at the rope and whine incessantly, so that in the end Big Joe would always take pity and go and untie her.

Then, one afternoon, Bertha went missing again. This time she did not come back. This time we could not find her. Charlie wasn't about. Mother and Big Joe went one way looking for her, down towards the river, and I went up into the woods, whistling for her, calling for her. There were deer to be found up in Ford's Cleave Wood, and badgers and foxes. It would be just the sort of place she'd go. I'd been an hour or more searching in the woods with not a sign of her. I was about to give up and go back — perhaps she'd gone home anyway by now, I thought — when I heard a shot ringing out across the valley. It came from somewhere higher in the woods. I ran up the track, ducking the low slung branches, leaping the badger holes, dreading, but already knowing what I would find.

As I came up the rise I could see ahead of me the chimney of Father's old shack, and then the shack itself at the side of the clearing. Outside lay Bertha, her tongue lolling, the grass beside her soaked with blood. The Colonel stood looking down at her, his shotgun in his hands. The door of the shack opened and Charlie and Molly were standing there frozen in disbelief and horror. Then Molly ran over to where Bertha lay and fell to her knees.

"Why?" she cried, looking up at the Colonel. "Why?"

NEARLY
FIVE TO ONE

There's a sliver of a moon out there, a new moon. I wonder if they're looking at it back home. Bertha used to howl at the moon, I remember. If I had a coin in my pocket, I'd turn it over and make a wish. When I was young I really believed in all those old tales. I wish I still could believe in them.

But I mustn't think like that. It's no good wishing for the moon, no good wishing for the impossible. Don't wish, Tommo. Remember. Remembrances are real.

❖   ❖   ❖

We buried Bertha the same day, where Big Joe always buried his creatures, where the mouse had been buried, at the bottom of the orchard. But this time we said no prayers. We laid no flowers. We sang no hymns. Somehow none of us had the heart for it. Perhaps we were all too angry to grieve. Walking back through the trees afterwards, Big Joe was pointing upwards and asking Mother if Bertha was up in Heaven now with Father. Mother said that she was. "When we die, Mother," Big Joe asked, "do we all go up there to Heaven?"

"Not the Colonel," Charlie muttered. "He'll go downstairs where he belongs, where he'll burn." Mother darted a reproving glance at him for that.

"Yes, Joe," she went on, her arm around him. "Bertha's up in Heaven. She's happy now."

That evening Big Joe went missing. None of us was that worried, not at first, not while it was still light. Big Joe would often go wandering off on his own from time to time — he'd always done that — but never at night, because Big Joe was frightened of the dark. Our first thought was to look down in the orchard by Bertha's grave, but he wasn't there. We called, but he didn't come. So, as darkness fell and he still had not come home, we knew there was something wrong. Mother sent Charlie and me out in different directions. I went down the lane calling for him all the way. I went as far as the brook, where I stood and listened for him, for his heavy stomping tread, for his singing. He sang differently when he was frightened, no tunes or songs, but instead a continuous wailing drone. But there was no drone to be heard, only the running of the brook, which always sounded louder at night. I knew Big Joe must be very frightened for it was by now quite dark. I made my way home, hoping against hope that either Charlie or Mother might have found him.

As I came into the house I could see neither of them had. They looked up hopefully at me as I came in. I shook my head. Out of the silence that followed Mother made up her mind what had to be done. We didn't have any choice, she said. All that mattered was finding Big Joe, and for that we needed more people. She would go up to the Big House right away to ask for the Colonel's help. She sent Charlie and me up to the village to raise the alarm. We knew the best place to go was the pub, that half the village would be in The Duke in the evening. They were singing when we got there, Farmer Cox in full voice. The hubbub and the singing took a while to die down as Charlie told them. By the time he had finished they were all listening in absolute silence. Afterwards, not one of them hesitated. They were putting on hats, shrugging on coats and heading homewards to search their farms, gardens and sheds. The vicar said he'd gather everyone he could in the village hall to organize a search around the village itself, and it was agreed the sounding of the church bell would be the signal that Big Joe had been found.

As everyone dispersed into the darkness outside The Duke, Molly came running up. She had just heard the news about Big Joe. It was her idea that he could be somewhere in the churchyard. I don't know why we hadn't thought of it before — it was always one of his favorite places. So the three of us made for the churchyard. We called for him. We looked behind every gravestone, up every tree. He was nowhere. All we heard was the wind sighing in the yew trees. All we saw were lights dancing through the village, down along the valley. Beyond, and as far as the dark horizon, the countryside was filled with pinpricks of moving lights. We knew then that Mother must have persuaded the Colonel to mobilize everyone on the estate to join in the search.

By dawn there was still no word of Big Joe, still no sign of him. The Colonel had called in the police, and as time passed everything was pointing towards the same dreadful conclusion. We saw the police searching the ponds and river banks with long poles — everyone knew Big Joe could not swim. That was when I first began to believe that the worst could really have happened. No one dared to voice this fear, but all of us were beginning to feel it, and we felt it in each other too.

We were searching over ground we had already searched several times. All other explanations for Big Joe's disappearance were being discounted one by one. If he had fallen asleep somewhere, surely he must have woken up by now. If he'd gone and got himself lost, surely, with all the hundreds of people out looking, someone would have found him by now. Everyone I met was grey and grim-faced. All tried their best to raise a smile, but no one could look me in the eye. I could see it wasn't just fear any more. It was worse. There was desperation in those faces, a feeling of complete hopelessness that they could not disguise however hard they tried.

Round about noon, thinking it was just possible Big Joe might somehow have found his way home on his own, we went back to check. We found Mother sitting there alone, clutching the arms of her chair and staring ahead of her. Charlie and I tried to raise her spirits, tried to reassure her as best we could. I don't think we were at all convincing. Charlie made her a cup of tea but Mother would not touch it. Molly sat at her feet and laid her head in her lap. A ghost of a smile came to Mother's face then. Molly could give comfort where we could give none.

Charlie and I left them there together and went outside into the garden. Clinging to what little hope we had left we tried to go back in time, to work out what might have been in

Big Joe's mind to make him go off like that. Perhaps it could help us to discover where he had gone if we understood why he had gone. Was he looking for something perhaps, something he'd lost? But what? Had he gone off to see someone? If so, who? There wasn't any doubt in our minds that his sudden disappearance was in some way connected to Bertha's death. The day before, both Charlie and I had felt like going up to the Big House and killing the Colonel for what he had done. Maybe, we thought, maybe Big Joe was feeling the same. Perhaps he had gone out to avenge Bertha's death. Perhaps he was skulking up at the Big House, in the attics, in the cellars, just waiting for his opportunity to strike. But we realized, even as we voiced them, that all such ideas were nothing but ridiculous nonsense. Big Joe didn't have it in him even to think of doing such a thing. He had never in his life been angry at anyone, not even the Wolfwoman — and after all, she'd given him reason enough and plenty. He could be hurt very easily, but he was never angry, and certainly never violent. Time and again Charlie and I would come up with a new scenario, a different reason for Big Joe's disappearance. But in the end we had to dismiss every one of them as fanciful.

Then we saw Molly come down the garden towards us. "I was just wondering," she said, "I was wondering where Big Joe would most want to be."

"What d'you mean?" Charlie asked.

"Well, I think he'd want to be wherever Bertha is. So he'd want to be in Heaven, wouldn't he? I mean, he thinks Bertha's up in Heaven, doesn't he? I heard your mother telling him. So if he wanted to be with Bertha, then he'd have to go up to Heaven, wouldn't he?"

I thought for one terrible moment that Molly was suggesting that Big Joe had killed himself so that he could go up to Heaven and be with Bertha. I didn't want to believe it, but it made a kind of dreadful sense. Then she explained.

"He told me once," Molly went on, "that your father was up in Heaven and could still see us easily from where he was. He was pointing upwards, I remember, and I didn't understand exactly what he was trying to tell me, not at first. I thought he was just pointing up at the sky in a general sort of a way, or at the birds maybe. But then he took my hand and made me point with him, to show me. We were pointing up at the church, at the top of the church tower. It sounds silly, but I think Big Joe believes that Heaven is at the top of the church tower. Has anyone looked up there?"

Even as she was speaking I remembered how Big Joe had pointed up at the church tower the day we had buried Father, how he'd looked back up at it over his shoulder as he walked away.

"You coming, Tommo?" said Charlie. "Moll, will you stay with Mother? We'll ring the bell if it's good news." We ran down through the orchard, scrambled through a hole in the hedge and set off across the fields towards the brook — it would be the quickest way up to the village. We splashed through the brook and raced across the water meadows and up the hill towards the church. Trying to keep up with Charlie was difficult. I kept looking up at the church tower as I ran, all the while urging my legs to keep going, to take me faster, all the while praying that Big Joe would be up there in his heaven.

Charlie reached the village before I did and was haring up the church path ahead of me when he slipped on the cobbles and fell heavily. He sat there cursing and clutching his leg until I caught up with him. Then he called, and I called, "Joe! Joe! Are you up there?" There was no reply.

"You go, Tommo," said Charlie, grimacing in agony. "I think I've done my ankle in." I opened the church door and walked into the silent dark of the church. I brushed past the bell ropes, and eased open the little belfry door. I could hear Charlie shouting, "Is he up there? Is he there?" I didn't answer. I began to climb the winding stairs. I'd been up into the belfry before, a while ago, when I was in Sunday school. I'd even sung up there in the choir one Ascension Day dawn, when I was little.

I dreaded those steps then and I hated them again now. The slit windows let in only occasional light. The walls were slimy about me, and the stairs uneven and slippery. The cold and the damp and the dark closed in on me and chilled me as I felt my way onwards and upwards. As I passed the silent hanging bells I hoped with all my heart that one of them would be ringing soon. Ninety-five steps I knew there were. With every step I was longing to reach the top, to breathe the bright air again, longing to find Big Joe.

The door to the tower was stiff and would not open. I pushed it hard, too hard, and it flew open, the wind catching it suddenly. I stepped out into the welcome warmth of day, dazzled by the light. At first glance I could see nothing. But then there he was. Big Joe was lying curled up under the shade of the parapet. He seemed fast asleep, his thumb in his mouth as usual. I didn't want to wake him too suddenly. When I touched his hand he did not wake. When I shook him gently by the shoulder he did not move. He was cold to my touch, and pale, deathly pale. I couldn't tell if he was breathing or not, and Charlie was calling up at me from below. I shook him again, hard this time, and screamed at him in my fear and panic. "Wake up, Joe. For God's sake, wake up!" I knew then that he wouldn't, that he'd come up here to die. He knew you had to die to go to Heaven, and Heaven was where he wanted to be, to be with Bertha again, with Father too.

When he stirred a moment later, I could hardly believe it. He opened his eyes. He smiled. "Ha, Tommo," he said. "Ung-wee. Ungwee." They were the most beautiful words I'd ever heard. I sprang to my feet and leaned out over the parapet. Charlie was down there on the church path looking up at me.

"We've found him, Charlie," I called down. "We've got him. He's up here. He's all right."

Charlie punched the air and yahooed again and again. He yahooed even louder when he saw Big Joe standing beside me and waving. "Charie!" he cried. "Charie!"

Charlie hopped and limped into the church, and only moments later the great tenor bell rang out over the village, scattering the roosting pigeons from the tower, and sending them wheeling out over the houses, over the fields. Like the pigeons, Big Joe and I were shocked at the violence of the sound. It blasted our ears, sent a tremor through the tower that we felt through the soles of our feet. Alarmed at all this thunderous clanging, Big Joe looked suddenly anxious, his hands clapped over his ears. But when he saw me laughing, he did the same. Then he hugged me, hugged me so tight I thought he was squeezing me half to death. And when he began singing his

Oranges and Lemons, I joined in, crying and singing at the same time.

I wanted him to come down with me, but Big Joe wanted to stay. He wanted to wave at everyone from the parapet. People were coming from all over: Mr. Munnings, Miss McAllister and all the children were streaming out through the school yard and up towards the church. We saw the Colonel, coming down the road in his car, and could just make out the Wolfwoman's bonnet beside him. Best of all we saw Mother and Molly on bicycles racing up the hill, waving at us. Still Charlie rang the bell and I could hear him yahooing down below between each dong, and imagined him hanging on to the rope and riding with it up in the air. Still Big Joe sang his song. And the swifts soared and swooped and screamed all around us, in the sheer joy of being alive, and celebrating, it seemed to me, that Big Joe was alive too.

TWENTY-EIGHT
MINUTES PAST ONE

I was once told in Sunday school that a church tower reaches up skywards because it is a promise of Heaven. Church towers are different in France. It was the first thing I noticed when I came here, when I changed my world of home for my world of war. In comparison the church towers at home seem almost squat, hiding themselves away in the folds of the fields. Here there are no folds in the fields, only wide open plains, scarcely a hill in sight. And instead of church towers they have spires that thrust themselves skywards like a child putting his hand up in class, longing to be noticed. But God, if there is one, notices nothing here. He has long since abandoned this place and all of us who live in it. There are not many steeples left now. I have seen the one in Albert, hanging down like a broken promise.

Now I come to think of it, it was a broken promise that brought me here, to France, and now to this barn. The mouse is back again. That's good.

There was a brief time just after we'd found Big Joe when all old hurts and grudges seemed suddenly to be forgiven and forgotten. Forgotten too, was all talk of the war in France. No one spoke of anything that day except our search for Big Joe and its happy outcome. Even the Colonel and the Wolfwoman were celebrating with the rest of us up in The Duke. Molly's mother and father were there too, celebrating with everyone else, and smiling — though being strict chapel people, they didn't touch a drop of drink. I'd never seen Molly's mother smile before that. And then the Colonel announced that he was paying for all the drinks. It wasn't long — it only took a couple of pints — before Farmer Cox began singing. He was still singing when we left; some of the songs were getting a bit rude by then. I was there outside The Duke when Mother went up and thanked the Colonel for his help. He offered us all a lift home in his Rolls Royce! The Peacefuls in the back of the Colonel's car, and the Wolfwoman in the front, being friendly! We couldn't believe it, not after all the bad blood between us over the years.

The Colonel broke the spell on the way home, talking about the war, and how the army should be using more cavalry over in France.

"Horses and guns," he said, "in that order. That's how we beat the Boers in South Africa. That's what they should be doing. If I were younger, I'd go myself. They'll soon be needing every horse they can find, Mrs. Peaceful, and every man too. It's not going at all well out there."

Mother thanked him again as he helped us out of the car outside our gate. The Colonel touched his hat and smiled. "Don't you go running off again, young man," he said to Big Joe. "You gave us all a terrible fright." And even the Wolfwoman waved at us almost cheerily as they drove off.

That night Big Joe began coughing. He'd caught a chill and it had gone to his lungs. He was in bed with a fever for weeks afterwards, and Mother hardly left his side, she was so worried.

By the time he was better, the whole episode of his disappearance had been forgotten, overtaken by news in the papers of a great and terrible battle on the Marne, where our armies were fighting the Germans to a standstill, trying desperately to halt their advance through France.

One evening, Charlie and I arrived home from work a little late, having stopped on the way for a drink at The Duke, as we often did. In those days, I remember, I had to pretend I liked the beer. The truth was I hated the stuff, but I loved the company. Charlie might have bossed me about on the farm, but after work, up at The Duke, he never treated me like the fifteen-year-old I was, though some of the others did. I couldn't have them knowing that I hated beer. So I'd force down a couple of pints with Charlie, and often left The Duke a little befuddled in the head. That was why I was woozy when we came home that evening. When I opened the door and saw Molly, sitting there on the floor with her head on Mother's lap, it seemed I was suddenly back to the day Big Joe had gone missing. Molly looked up at us, and I could see that she had been crying, and that this time it was Mother doing the comforting.

"What is it?" Charlie asked. "What's happened?"

"You may well ask, Charlie Peaceful," Mother said. She didn't sound at all pleased to see us. I wondered at first if she had seen we'd been drinking. Then I noticed a leather suitcase under the windowsill, and Molly's coat over the back of Father's fireside chair.

"Molly's come to stay," Mother went on. "They've thrown her out, Charlie. Her mother and father have thrown her out, and it's your fault."

"No!" Molly cried. "Don't say that. It isn't his fault. It's no one's fault." She ran over to Charlie and threw herself into his arms.

"What's happened, Moll?" asked Charlie. "What's going on?"

Molly was shaking her head as she wept uncontrollably now on his shoulder. He looked at Mother.

"What's going on, Charlie, is that she's going to have your baby," she said. "They packed her case, put her out of the door and told her never to come back. They never want to see her again. She had nowhere else to go, Charlie. I said she was family, that she belongs with us now, that she can stay as long as she likes."

It seemed an age before Charlie said anything. I saw his face go through all manner of emotions: incomprehension, bewilderment, outrage, through all these at once, and then at last to resolve. He held Molly away from him now and brushed away her tears with his thumb as he looked steadily into her eyes. When he spoke at last, it wasn't to Molly, but to Mother. "You shouldn't have said that to Moll, Mother," he spoke slowly, almost sternly. Then he began to smile. "That was for me to say. It's our baby, my baby, and Moll's my girl. So I should have said it. But I'm glad you said it all the same."

After that Molly became even more one of us than she had been before. I was both overjoyed and miserable at the same time. Molly and Charlie knew how I must have felt, I think, but they never spoke of it and neither did I.

They were married up in the church a short time later. It was a very empty church. There was no one there except the vicar and the four of us, and the vicar's wife sitting at the back. Everyone knew about Molly's baby by now, and because of that the vicar had only agreed to marry them on certain conditions: that no bells were to be rung and no hymns to be sung. He rushed through the marriage service as if he wanted to be somewhere else. There was no wedding feast afterwards, only a cup of tea and some fruit cake when we got home.

Shortly afterwards, Mother received a letter from the Wolfwoman saying it had been a marriage of shame; how she had thought of dismissing Molly and only decided against it because, whilst Molly was clearly a weak and immoral girl, she felt she could not in all conscience punish Molly for something that she was sure was much more Charlie's fault than hers, and that anyway Molly had already been punished enough for her wickedness. Mother read the letter out loud

to all of us, then scrunched it up and threw it into the fire —
where it belonged, she said.

I moved into Big Joe's room and slept with him in his bed,
which wasn't easy because he was big and the bed very narrow.
He muttered to himself loudly in his dreams, and tossed and
turned almost constantly. But, as I lay awake at nights, that
was not what troubled me most. In the next room slept the
two people I most loved in all the world who, in finding each
other, had deserted me. Sometimes, in the dead of night, I
thought of them lying in each other's arms and I wanted to
hate them. But I couldn't. All I knew was that I had no place
at home any more, that I would be better off away, and away
from them in particular.

I tried never to be alone with Molly for I did not know
what to say to her any more. I didn't stop to drink with Charlie
any more at The Duke, for the same reason. On the farm, I
took every opportunity that came my way to work on my
own, so as to be nowhere near him. I volunteered for any
fetching and carrying that had to be done away from the
farm. Farmer Cox seemed more than happy for me to do that.
He was always sending me off with the horse and cart on
some errand or other: bringing back feed from the merchants
maybe, fetching the seed potatoes, or perhaps taking a pig to

market to sell for him. Whatever it was, I took my time about it and Farmer Cox never seemed to notice. But Charlie did. He said I was skiving off work, but he knew that all I was doing was avoiding him. We knew each other so well. We never argued, not really; perhaps it was because neither of us wanted to hurt the other. We both knew enough hurt had been done already, that more would only widen the rift between us and neither of us wanted that.

It was while I was off "skiving" in Hatherleigh market one morning that I came face to face with the war for the first time, a war that until now had seemed unreal and distant to all of us, a war only in newspapers and on posters. I'd just sold Farmer Cox's two old rams, and got a good price for them too, when I heard the sound of a band coming down the High Street, drums pounding, bugles blaring. Everyone in the market went running, and so did I.

As I came round the corner I saw them. Behind the band there must have been a couple of dozen soldiers, splendid in their scarlet uniforms. They marched past me, arms swinging in perfect time, buttons and boots shining, the sun glinting on their bayonets. They were singing along with the band: *It's a long way to Tipperary, it's a long way to go.* And I remember thinking it was a good thing Big Joe wasn't there, because he'd have been bound to join in with his *Oranges and Lemons.*

Children were stomping alongside them, some in paper hats, some with wooden sticks over their shoulders. And there were women throwing flowers, roses mostly, that were falling at the soldiers' feet. But one of them landed on a soldier's tunic and somehow stuck there. I saw him smile at that.

Like everyone else, I followed them round the town and up into the square. The band played *God Save the King* and then, with the Union Jack fluttering behind him, the first sergeant major I'd ever set eyes on got up on to the steps of the cross, slipped his stick smartly under his arm, and spoke to us, his voice unlike any voice I'd heard before: rasping, commanding.

"I shan't beat about the bush, ladies and gentlemen," he began. "I shan't tell you it's all tickety-boo out there in France — there's been too much of that nonsense already in my view. I've been there. I've seen it for myself. So I'll tell you straight. It's no picnic. It's hard slog, that's what it is, hard slog. Only one question to ask yourself about this war. Who would you rather see marching through your streets? Us lot or the Hun? Make up your minds. Because, mark my words, ladies and gentlemen, if we don't stop them out in France the Germans will be here, right here in Hatherleigh, right here on your doorstep."

I could feel the silence all around.

"They'll come marching through here burning your houses, killing your children, and yes, violating your women. They've beaten brave little Belgium, swallowed her up in one gulp. And now they've taken a fair slice of France too. I'm here to tell you that unless we beat them at their own game, they'll gobble us up as well." His eyes raked over us. "Well? Do you want the Hun here? Do you?"

"No!" came the shout, and I was shouting along with them.

"Shall we knock the stuffing out of them then?"

"Yes!" we roared in unison.

The sergeant major nodded. "Good. Very good. Then we shall need you." He was pointing his stick now into the crowd, picking out the men. "You, and you and you." He was looking straight at me now, into my eyes. "And you too, my lad!"

Until that very moment it had honestly never occurred to me that what he was saying had anything to do with me. I had been an onlooker. No longer.

"Your king needs you. Your country needs you. And all the brave lads out in France need you too." His face broke into a smile as he fingered his immaculate mustache. "And remember one thing, lads — and I can vouch for this — all the girls love a soldier."

The ladies in the crowd all laughed and giggled at that. Then the sergeant major returned the stick under his arm.

"So, who'll be the first brave lad to come up and take the king's shilling?"

No one moved. No one spoke up. "Who'll lead the way? Come along now. Don't let me down, lads. I'm looking for boys with hearts of oak, lads who love their king and their country, brave boys who hate the lousy Hun."

That was the moment the first one stepped forward, flourishing his hat as he pushed his way through the cheering crowd. I knew him at once from school. It was big Jimmy Parsons. I hadn't seen him for a while, not since his family had moved away from the village. He was even bigger than I remembered, fuller in the face and neck, and redder too. He was showing off now just like he always had done in the school yard. Egged on by the crowd, others soon followed.

Suddenly someone prodded me hard in the small of my back. It was a toothless old lady pointing at me with her crooked finger. "Go on, son," she croaked. "You go and fight. It's every man's duty to fight when his country calls, that's what I say. Go on. Y'ain't a coward, are you?"

Everyone seemed to be looking at me then, urging me on, their eyes accusing me as I hesitated. The toothless old lady jabbed me again, and then she was pushing me forward. "Y'ain't a coward, are you? Y'ain't a coward?" I didn't run, not at first. I sidled away from her slowly, and then backed out of the crowd, hoping no one would notice me. But she did. "Chicken!" she screamed after me. "Chicken!" Then I did run. I ran helter-skelter down the deserted High Street, her words still ringing in my ears.

As I drove the cart out of the market, I heard the band strike up again in the square, heard the echoing thump thump of the big bass drum calling me back to the flag. Filled with shame, I kept on going. All the way back to the farm I thought about the toothless old lady, about what she had said, what the sergeant major had said. I thought about how fine and manly the men looked in their bright uniforms, how Molly would admire me, might even love me, if I joined up and came home in my scarlet uniform, how proud Mother would be, and Big Joe. By the time I was unhitching the horse back at the farm, I was quite determined that I would do it. I would be a soldier. I would go to France and, like the sergeant major said, kick the stuffing out of the lousy Germans. I made up my mind I would break the news to everyone at supper. I couldn't wait to tell them, to see the look on their faces.

We'd barely sat down before I began. "I was in Hatherleigh this morning," I said. "Mr. Cox sent me to market."

"Skiving as usual," Charlie muttered into his soup.

I ignored him and went on. "The army was there, Mother.

Recruiting, they were. Jimmy Parsons joined up. Lots of others too."

"More fool them," Charlie said. "I'm not going, not ever. I'll shoot a rat because it might bite me. I'll shoot a rabbit because I can eat it. Why would I ever want to shoot a German? Never even met a German."

Mother picked up my spoon and handed it to me. "Eat," she said, and she patted my arm. "And don't worry about it, Tommo, they can't make you go. You're too young anyway."

"I'm nearly sixteen," I said.

"You've got to be seventeen," said Charlie. "They won't let you join unless you are. They don't want boys."

So I ate my soup and said no more about it. I was disappointed at first that I hadn't had my big moment, but as I lay in bed that night I was secretly more than a little relieved that I wouldn't be going off to the war, and that by the time I was seventeen it would all be over anyway, as like as not.

A few weeks later the Colonel paid Mother a surprise visit, whilst Charlie and I were out at work. We didn't hear about it until we got home in the evening and Molly told us. I thought something strange was going on, as Mother was unusually preoccupied and quiet at supper. She wouldn't even answer Big Joe's questions. Then when Molly got up, saying she felt like a walk, and suggested both Charlie and I come with her, I knew for sure something was up. It was a very long time since we'd been out together, just the three of us. If Charlie had asked me, I'd have said no for sure. But it was always more difficult for me to refuse Molly.

We went down to the brook, just like we'd done in the old days whenever we'd wanted to be alone together, where Molly and I had met up so often when I'd been their go-between postman. Molly didn't tell us until we were sitting on either side of her on the river bank, until she had taken each of us by the hand.

"I'm breaking a promise I made to your mother," she began. "I so much don't want to tell you this, but I must. You have to know what's going on. It's the Colonel. He came in and told her this morning. He said he was only doing what he called his 'patriotic duty.' He told us that the war was going badly for us, that the country was crying out for men. So he's decided that now is the time for every able-bodied man who lives or works on his estate, everyone who can be spared, to volunteer, to go off to the war and do his bit for king and country. The estate will just have to manage without them for a while." I felt Molly's grip tighten on my hand, and a tremor come into her voice. "He said you've got to go, Charlie, or else he won't let us stay on in the cottage. Your mother protested all she could, but he wouldn't listen. He just lost his temper. He'll put us out, Charlie, and he won't go on employing your mother or me unless you go."

"He wouldn't do that, Moll. It's just a threat," Charlie said. "He can't do it. He just can't."

"He would," Molly replied, "and he can. You know he can. And when the Colonel gets it into his head to do something, and he's in the mood to do it, he will. Look what he did to Bertha. He means it, Charlie."

"But the Colonel promised," I said. "And his wife did too, before she died. She said she wanted Mother looked after. And the Colonel said we could stay on in the cottage. Mother told us."

"Your mother reminded him of that," Molly replied. "And d'you know what he said? He said it had never been a promise as such, only his wife's wish, and that anyway the war had changed everything. He was making no exceptions. Charlie has to join up or we'll be out of the cottage at the end of the month."

We sat there holding hands, Molly's head on Charlie's shoulder, as evening fell around us. Molly was sobbing quietly from time to time but none of us spoke. We didn't need to. We all knew there was no way out of this, that the war was breaking us apart, and that all our lives would be changed forever. But at that moment, I treasured Molly's hand in mine, treasured this last time together.

Suddenly, Charlie broke the silence. "I'll be honest, Moll," he said. "It's been bothering me a lot just lately. Don't get me wrong. I don't want to go. But I've seen the lists in the papers — y'know, all the killed and the wounded. Poor beggars. Pages of them. It hardly seems right, does it, me being here, enjoying life, while they're over there. It's not all bad, Moll. I saw Benny Copplestone yesterday. He was sporting his uniform up at the pub. He's back on leave. He's been a year or more out in Belgium. He says it's all right. 'Cushy,' he called it. He says we've got the Germans on the run now. One big push, he reckons, and they'll all be running back to Berlin with their tails between their legs, and then all our boys can come home."

He paused, and kissed Molly on her forehead. "Anyway, it looks like I haven't got much choice, have I, Moll?"

"Oh Charlie," Molly whispered. "I don't want you to go."

"Don't worry, girl," Charlie said. "With a bit of luck I'll be back to wet the baby's head. And Tommo will look after you. He'll be the man about the place, won't you, Tommo? And if that silly old fart of a Colonel sticks his lousy head in our front door again when I'm gone, shoot the bastard, Tommo, like he shot Bertha." And I knew he was only half-joking too.

I don't believe I even thought about what I said next. "I'm not staying," I told them. "I'm coming with you, Charlie."

They both tried all they could to dissuade me. They argued, they bullied, but I would not be put off, not this time. I was too young, Charlie said. I said I was sixteen in a couple of weeks and as tall as he was, that all I had to do was shave and talk deeper and I could easily be taken for seventeen. Mother wouldn't let me go, Molly said. I said I'd run away, that she couldn't lock me up.

"And who'll be there to look after us if you both go?" Molly was pleading with me now.

"Who would you rather I look after, Molly," I replied. "All of you at home who can perfectly well look after yourselves? Or Charlie, who's always getting himself into nasty scrapes, even at home?" When they had no answer to this, they knew I'd won, and I knew it too. I was going to fight in the war with Charlie. Nothing and no one could stop me now.

I've had two long years to think on why I decided like that, on the spur of the moment, to go with Charlie. In the end I suppose it was because I couldn't bear the thought of being apart from him. We'd lived our lives always together, shared everything, even our love for Molly. Maybe I just didn't want him to have this adventure without me. And then there was that spark in me newly kindled by those scarlet soldiers marching bravely up the High Street in Hatherleigh, the steady march of their feet, the drums and bugles resounding through the town, the sergeant major's stirring call to arms. Perhaps he had awoken in me feelings I never realized I'd had before, and that I had certainly never talked about. It was true that I did love all that was familiar to me. I loved what I knew, and what I knew was my family, and Molly, and the countryside I'd grown up in. I did not want any enemy soldier ever setting foot on our soil, on my place. I would do all I could to stop him and to protect the people I loved. And I would be doing it with Charlie. Deep down though, I knew that, more than Charlie, more than my country or the band or the sergeant major, it was that toothless old woman taunting me in the square. "Y'ain't a coward, are you? Y'ain't a coward?"

The truth was that I wasn't sure I wasn't, and I needed to find out.

I had to prove myself. I had to prove myself to myself.

Two days later, two days of parrying Mother's many attempts to keep me from going, we all went off together to Eggesford Junction Station, where Charlie and I were to catch the train to Exeter. Big Joe had not been told anything about us going off to war. We were going away for a while, and we'd be back soon.

We didn't tell him the truth, but we told him no lies either. Mother and Molly tried not to cry because of him. So did we.

"Look after Charlie for me, Tommo," Molly said. "And look after yourself too." I could feel the swell of her belly against me as we hugged.

Mother told me to promise to keep clean, to be good, to write home and to come home. Then Charlie and I were on the train — the first train we'd ever been on in our lives, and we were leaning out of the window and waving, only pulling back spluttering and coughing when we were engulfed suddenly in a cloud of sooty smoke. When it cleared and we looked out again, the station was already out of sight. We sat down opposite each other.

"Thanks, Tommo," said Charlie.

"For what?" I said.

"You know," he replied, and we both looked out of the window. There was no more to say about it. A heron lifted off the river and accompanied us for a while before veering away from us and landing high in the trees. A startled herd of Ruby Red cows scattered as we passed by, tails high as they ran. Then we were in a tunnel, a long dark tunnel filled with din and smoke and blackness. It seems like I've been in that tunnel every day since. So Charlie and I went rattling off to war. It all seems a very long time ago now, a lifetime.

FOURTEEN MINUTES PAST TWO

I keep checking the time. I promised myself I wouldn't, but I can't seem to help myself. Each time I do it, I put the watch to my ear and listen for the tick. It's still there, softly slicing away the seconds, then the minutes, then the hours. It tells me there are three hours and forty-six minutes left. Charlie told me once this watch would never stop, never let me down, unless I forgot to wind it. The best watch in the world, he said, a wonderful watch. But it isn't. If it was such a wonderful watch it would do more than simply keep the time — any old watch can do that. A truly wonderful watch would *make* the time. Then, if it stopped, time itself would have to stand still, then this night would never have to end and morning could never come. Charlie often told me we were living on borrowed time out here. I don't want to borrow any more time. I want time to stop so that tomorrow never comes, so that dawn will never happen.

I listen to my watch again, to Charlie's watch. Still ticking. Don't listen, Tommo. Don't look. Don't think. Only remember.

❖   ❖   ❖

"Stand still! Look to your front, Peaceful, you horrible little man!". . ."Stomach in, chest out, Peaceful.". . ."Down in that mud, Peaceful, where you belong, you nasty little worm. Down!". . ."God, Peaceful, is that the best they can send us these days? Vermin, that's what you are. Lousy vermin, and I've got to make a soldier of you."

Of all the names Sergeant "Horrible" Hanley bellowed out across the parade ground at Etaples when we first came to France, Peaceful was by far the most frequent. There were two Peacefuls in the company of course, and that made a difference, but it wasn't the main reason. Right from the very start Sergeant Hanley had it in for Charlie. And that was because Charlie just wouldn't jump through hoops like the rest of us, and that was because Charlie wasn't frightened of him, like the rest of us were.

Before we ever came to Etaples, all of us, including Charlie and me, had had an easy ride, a gentle enough baptism into the life of soldiering. In fact we'd had several weeks of little else but larks and laughter. On the train to Exeter, Charlie said we could easily pass for twins, that I'd have to watch my step, drop my voice, and behave like a seventeen-year-old from now on. When the time came, in front of the recruiting sergeant at the regimental depot, I stood as tall as I could and Charlie spoke up for me, so my voice wouldn't betray me. "I'm Charlie Peaceful, and he's Thomas Peaceful. We're twins and we're volunteering."

"Date of birth?"

"5th October," said Charlie.

"Both of you?" asked the recruiting sergeant, eyeing me a little, I thought.

"Course," Charlie replied, lying easily, "only I'm older than him by one hour." And that was that. Easy. We were in.

The boots they gave us were stiff and far too big — they hadn't got any smaller sizes. So Charlie and I and the others clomped about like clowns, clowns in tin hats and khaki. The uniforms didn't fit either, so we swapped about until they did. There were some faces from home we recognized amongst the hundreds of strangers. Nipper Martin, a little fellow with sticking-out ears, who grew turnips on his father's farm in Dolton, and who played a wicked game of skittles up at The Duke. There was Pete Bovey, thatcher and cider drinker from Dolton too, red-faced and with hands like spades, who we'd often seen around the village in Iddesleigh, thumping away at the thatch, high up on someone's roof. With us too, was little Les James from school, son of Bob James, village rat catcher and wart charmer. He had inherited his father's gifts with rats and warts and he always claimed to be able to know whether it was going to rain or not the next day. He was usually right too. He always had a nervous tick in one eye that I could never stop looking at when we were in class together.

At training camp on Salisbury Plain, living cheek by jowl, we all got to know each other fast, though not necessarily to like one another — that came later. And we got to know our parts too, how to make believe we were soldiers. We learnt how to wear our khaki costumes — I never did get to wear the scarlet uniform I'd been hoping for — how to iron creases in and iron wrinkles out, how to patch and mend our socks, how to polish our buttons and badges and boots. We learnt how to march up and down in time, how to about-turn without bumping into one another, how to flick our heads right and salute whenever we saw an officer. Whatever we did, we did together, in time — all except for little Les James, who could never swing his arms in time with the rest of us, no matter how much the sergeants and corporals bellowed at him. His legs and arms stepped and swung in time with each other, and with no one else, and that was all there was to it. He didn't seem to mind how often they shouted at him that he had two left feet. It gave us all something to laugh about. We did a lot of laughing in those early days.

They gave us rifles and packs and trenching shovels. We learnt to run up hills with heavy packs, and how to shoot straight. Charlie didn't have to be taught. On the rifle range he proved to be far and away the best shot in the company. When they gave him his red marksman's badge I was so proud of him. He was pretty pleased himself too. Even with the bayonets it was still a game of make-believe. We'd have to charge forward screaming whatever obscenities we knew — and I didn't know many, not then — at the straw-filled dummies. We'd plunge our bayonets in up to the hilt, swearing and cursing the filthy Hun as we stabbed him, twisting the blade and pulling it out as we'd been taught. "Go for the stomach, Peaceful. Nothing to get hung up on in there. Jab. Twist. Out."

Everything in the army had to be done in lines or rows. We slept in long lines of tents, sat on privies in rows. Not even the privy was private, I learnt that very quickly. In fact nowhere was private any more. We lived every moment of every day together, and usually in lines. We lined up together for shaves, for food, for inspections. Even when we dug trenches, they had to be in lines, straight trenches with straight edges, and we had to dig fast too, one company in competition with another. We poured sweat, our backs ached, our hands were permanently raw with blisters. "Faster!" the corporals shouted. "Deeper! You want to get your head blowed off, Peaceful?"

"No, Corporal."

"You want to get your arse blowed off, Peaceful?"

"No, Corporal."

"You want to get your nuts blowed off, Peaceful?"

"No, Corporal."

"Then dig, you lazy beggars, dig, 'cos when you get out there, that's all you've got to hide in, God's good earth. And when they whizzbangs come over I'm telling you you'll always wish you'd dug deeper. The deeper you dig the longer you'll live. I know, I've been there."

No matter what the officers and NCOs told us of the hardships and dangers of trench warfare, we still all believed we were simply in some kind of rehearsal, actors in costume. We had to play our part, dress our part, but in the end it

III

would only be a play. That was what we tried to believe — if ever we spoke about it, that is. But the truth was that we didn't speak of it much. I think we didn't dare because deep down we all knew and we all trembled, and were trying to deny it or disguise it or both.

I remember we were on exercise in the hills, lying there on our backs in the sunshine one morning, when Pete sat up suddenly. "Hear that?" he said. "It's guns, from over in France, real guns." We sat up and listened. We heard it. Some said it was distant thunder. But we heard it all right. We saw the sudden fear in each other's eyes and knew it for what it was.

But that same afternoon we were back to play-acting, war games in full pack, attacking some distant "enemy" copse. When the whistles blew we climbed out of our trenches and walked forward, bayonets fixed. Then on a bellowed command we threw ourselves face down and crawled on through the long grass. The ground under us was still warm with summer, and there were buttercups. I thought of Molly then and Charlie and the buttercups in the water meadows back home. A bee, heavy with pollen and still greedy for more, clover-hopped in front of me as I crawled. I remember I spoke to him. "We're much alike, bee, you and me," I said. "You may carry your pack underneath you and your rifle may stick out of your bottom. But you and me, bee, are much alike." The bee must have taken offense at this, because he took off and flew away. I lay where I was, propped up on my elbows, and watched him go, until my thoughts were rudely interrupted by the corporal.

"What d'you think you're on, Peaceful, a bloody picnic? On your feet!"

In those first few weeks in uniform I hardly had time to miss anyone, not even Molly, though I thought of her often, and Mother and Big Joe. But they were only ever fleeting thoughts. Charlie and I rarely talked of home — we were hardly ever alone together anyway. We'd even stopped cursing the Colonel by now. There didn't seem any point, not any more. It was a hateful thing he'd done, but it was a done thing. We were soldiers now, and it wasn't bad, so far. In fact, despite all the lining up and the bellowing, it was turning out to be a lark, a real lark. Charlie and I wrote cheery letters home — most of his were to Molly, all of mine to Mother and Big Joe. We read them aloud to each other, those bits we wanted to share anyway. We weren't allowed to say where we were or anything about the training, but we always found plenty to tell them, plenty to brag about, plenty to ask about. We told them the truth, that we were having a good time — eating well and being good — mostly. But the moment we got on the ship for France the good times ended. Little Les

James said he smelled a storm in the air, and as usual he was right.

There wasn't a man on board that ship that didn't want to die before he ever got to France. Most of us, Charlie and me included, had never seen the sea before, much less the heaving grey waves of the English Channel, and we lurched about the deck like drunken ghosts longing only to be released from our agony. Charlie and I were vomiting over the side when a seaman came up to us, clapped us heartily on the back and told us that if we were going to die we'd feel much better doing it down below in the hold with the horses. So Charlie and I staggered down the gangways until we found ourselves deep in the bowels of the ship and in amongst the terrified horses, who seemed happy to have someone for company as we crawled in and curled up in their straw, too close to their hooves for safety, but feeling too ill to care. The seaman was right. Down here the ship seemed to roll much less, and despite the stifling stench of oil and horse dung we began to feel better almost at once.

When at long last the engines finally stopped we went up on deck and looked out at France for the first time. The French gull that hovered overhead, eyeing me with deep suspicion, looked much like every gull I'd seen following the plow back at home. Every voice I heard on the quayside below was English. Every uniform and every helmet was like our own. Then, as we came down the gangplank into the fresh morning air, we saw them, the lines of walking wounded shuffling along the quay towards us, some with their eyes bandaged, holding on to the shoulder of the one in front. Others lay on stretchers. One of them, puffing on a cigarette between pale parched lips, looked up at me out of sunken yellow eyes. "G'luck lads," he cried as we passed. "Give 'em what for." The rest stayed silent and their staring silence spoke to each of us as we formed up and marched out of town. We all knew then that the larking and the play-acting were over. From that moment none of us doubted the seriousness of what this would be about. It was our lives we would be acting out over here, and for many of us, our deaths.

If any of us had any last lingering delusions then they were very soon dispelled by our first sight of the vast training camp at Etaples. The camp stretched away as far as the eye could see, a tented city, and everywhere I looked there were soldiers drilling — marching, doubling, crawling, wheeling, saluting, presenting arms. I had never in my life seen such a bustle of people, never heard such a racket of humanity. The air echoed with the din of barked orders and shrieked obscenities. That was when we first came across Sergeant Horrible Hanley, our chief scourge and tormentor over the coming weeks, who was to do his utmost to make all our lives a misery.

From the moment we saw him most of us lived in dread of him. He was not a big man, but he had eyes of steel that bore into us, and a lashing snarl in his voice that terrified us. We just buckled under and did what he wanted us to. It was the only way to survive. However much he doubled us up hills with stones in our packs, however much he made us throw ourselves down in the freezing mud and crawl through it, we did it, and with a will too. We knew that anything less — to protest, to complain, to talk back, even to look him in the eye — would be to draw down upon us even more fury, even more pain, even more punishment. We knew because we saw what happened to Charlie. Charlie wouldn't even go along with his little jokes. It was this that got him into trouble in the first place.

It was a Sunday morning and we were being inspected before a church parade when Sergeant Hanley found fault with Charlie's cap badge. He said it was crooked. Nose to nose, Hanley bellowed into Charlie's face. I was in the rank behind Charlie, but even there I could feel the spray from Hanley's spittle. "You know what you are? You're a blot on creation, Peaceful. What are you?"

Charlie thought for a moment and then replied in a clear,

firm voice, and utterly without fear: "Happy to be here, Sergeant."

Hanley looked taken aback. We all knew the answer Hanley was looking for. He asked again. "You're a blot on creation. What are you?"

"Like I said, Sergeant, happy to be here." Charlie just would not give Hanley the satisfaction of playing his game, no matter how often Hanley asked, nor how loud he shouted. For that Charlie was put on extra sentry duty, so that night after night Charlie hardly got any sleep. Hanley never let up after that, never missed an opportunity to pick on Charlie and punish him.

There were some in the company who didn't at all like what Charlie was doing, Pete amongst them. He said Charlie was stirring Hanley up unnecessarily, and was making things difficult for the rest of us. I've got to say I half agreed with them — though I didn't tell them that, and I certainly didn't tell Charlie. It was quite true that Hanley was giving our company in particular a lot of grief, and it was obvious this was because he had a vendetta against Charlie. Charlie was swiping at the wasp, and the wasp wasn't just stinging him, he was stinging all of us. Charlie was beginning to be thought of as a bit of a liability in the company, a bit of a Jonah. No one said as much to him — they all liked and respected Charlie too much — but Pete and Little Les and Nipper Martin did come to me on the quiet, and asked me to talk to him. I tried as best I could to warn Charlie. "He's like Mr. Munnings back at school, Charlie. Our lord and master, remember? Hanley's our lord and master out here. You can't fight him."

"But that doesn't mean I have to lie down and let him walk all over me," he said. "I'll be all right, you'll see. You look after yourself. You watch your back. He's got his eye on you, Tommo, I've seen him." That was typical Charlie. I was trying to warn him, and he just turned the whole thing around and ended up warning me.

It was a little enough thing that sparked it off, a dirty rifle barrel. Thinking back now I know for sure Hanley must have done it quite deliberately, to provoke Charlie. Everyone knew by now that I was Charlie's younger brother, and a year too young to enlist. We'd long ago given up the pretense of being twins. After we'd first met up with Pete and Little Les and Nipper from home, we'd had to come clean about it, and by then it didn't much matter. There were dozens of others underage in the regiment, and everyone knew it. After all, they needed all the men they could get. The other lads teased me about it, about having a chin like a baby's bottom and about my not needing to shave, about my squeaky voice too. But they all knew that Charlie was looking out for me. If ever the teasing got a bit out of hand, Charlie would give them a little look and it would stop. He never nannied me, but everyone knew he'd stick by me no matter what.

Hanley was nasty but he wasn't stupid. He must have sensed it too, and that was why he began picking on me as well. I'd had plenty of practice at putting up with this kind of thing back at school with Mr. Munnings, but Horrible Hanley was a tormentor in a class of his own. He found excuse after excuse to pick on me and punish me. Worn down by extra drills and sentry duty, I was very soon exhausted. The more exhausted I became the more mistakes I made, and the more mistakes I made, the more Hanley punished me.

We'd been drilling one morning, and were stood to attention in three ranks, when he grabbed my rifle. Looking down the barrel, Hanley pronounced it "dirty." I knew the punishment, we all did: five times doubling around the parade ground holding your rifle above your head. After only two circuits I just could not keep my rifle up there any more. My arms buckled at the elbows, and Hanley bellowed at me: "Every time you let that rifle fall, Peaceful, you begin the punishment again. Five more, Peaceful."

My head was swimming. I was staggering now, not running, and barely able to keep upright. My back was on fire with pain. I simply hadn't the strength to lift the rifle above my head at all. I remember hearing a shout, knowing it was Charlie, and wondering why he was shouting. Then I passed out. When I woke in my tent they told me what had happened. Charlie had broken ranks and run at Hanley, screaming at him. He hadn't actually hit him, but he had stood there nose to nose with Hanley, telling him exactly what he thought of him. They said it was magnificent, that everyone cheered when he'd finished. But Charlie had been marched off to the guardroom under arrest.

The next day, in heavy rain, the whole battalion was paraded to witness Charlie's punishment. He was brought out and lashed to a gun wheel. Field Punishment Number One, they called it. The brigadier in command sat high on his horse and said that this should be a warning to all of us, that Private Peaceful had got off lightly, that insubordination in time of war could be seen as mutiny, and that mutiny, was punishable by death, by the firing squad. All day long Charlie was lashed there in the rain, legs apart, arms spread-eagled. As we marched past him, Charlie smiled at me. I tried to smile back, but no smile came, only tears. He seemed to me like Jesus hanging on the cross in the church back home in Iddesleigh. And I thought then of the hymn we used to sing in Sunday school, *What a friend we have in Jesus,* and sang it to myself only to banish my tears as I marched. I remembered

Molly singing it down in the orchard when we buried Big Joe's mouse, and as I remembered I found myself involuntarily changing the words, changing Jesus into Charlie. I sang it to myself under my breath as we were marched away. "What a friend I have in Charlie."

A MINUTE
PAST THREE

I dropped off to sleep. I've lost precious minutes — I don't know how many, but they are minutes I can never have back. I should be able by now to fight off sleep. I've done it often enough on lookout in the trenches, but then I had cold or fear or both as my wakeful companions. I long for that moment of surrender to sleep, just to drift away into the warmth of nothingness. Resist it, Tommo, resist it. After this night is over, then you can drift away, then you can sleep forever, for nothing will ever matter again. Sing *Oranges and Lemons*. Go on. Sing

it. Sing it like Big Joe does, over and over again. That'll keep
you awake.

Oranges and Lemons, say the bells of St. Clements,
You owe me five farthings, say the bells of St. Martins.
When will you pay me? say the bells of Old Bailey.
When I grow rich, say the bells of Shoreditch.
When will that be? say the bells of Stepney.
I'm sure I don't know, says the great bell at Bow.
Here comes a candle to light you to bed,
And here comes a chopper to chop off your head.

❖   ❖   ❖

They tell us we're going up to the front, and we're all relieved.
We are leaving Etaples and Sergeant Hanley forever, we hope.
We're leaving France and marching into Belgium, singing as
we go. Captain Wilkes likes us to sing. Good for morale, he
says, and he's right too. The more we sing the more cheery we
become, and that's in spite of all we see — the shell-shattered
villages we march through, the field hospitals we pass, the
empty coffins waiting. The captain was a choirmaster and a
teacher back home in Salisbury, so he knows what he's doing.
We hope he'll know what he's doing when we get to the

trenches. It's difficult to believe he and Sergeant Horrible Hanley are in the same army, on the same side. We have never come across anyone who treats us with such kindness and consideration. As Charlie says, "he treats us right." So we treat him right too, except that is for Nipper Martin who ribs him whenever he can. Nipper can be like that, a bit mean sometimes. He's the only one who still keeps on about my squeaky voice.

"Are we downhearted? No! Then let your voices ring and altogether sing: Are we downhearted? No." We sing out and march with a new spring in our step. And when that finishes and there's just the sound of marching feet Charlie starts up with *Oranges and Lemons*, which makes us all laugh, the captain too. I join in and soon they're all singing along. No one knows why we sing it of course. It's a secret between Charlie and me, and I know as we sing that he's thinking of Big Joe and home, as I am.

The captain has told us we're going to a sector that's been quiet for a while now, that things shouldn't be too bad. We're happy about that of course, but we honestly don't care that much. Nothing could be worse than what we've just left. We pass a battery of heavy guns, the gunners sitting round a table playing cards. The guns are silent now, their barrels gaping at the enemy. I look where they point but can see no enemy. All

I have seen of our enemy so far is a huddle of ragged prisoners sheltering from the rain under a tree as we marched past, their grey uniforms caked in mud. Some of them were smiling. One of them even waved and called out: "Hello, Tommy."

"He's talking to you," said Charlie laughing. So I waved back. They seemed much like us, only dirtier.

Two airplanes circle like buzzards in the distance. As they come closer I see they are not circling at all, but chasing one another. They are still too far away for us to see which of them is ours. We make up our minds it is the smaller one and cheer for him madly, and I'm wondering suddenly if the pilot from the yellow plane that landed in the water meadows that day might be up there in our plane. I can almost taste the humbugs he gave us as I watch them. I lose them in the sun, and then the smaller one spirals earthwards and our cheering is instantly silenced.

At rest camp they give us our first letters. Charlie and I lie in our tent and read them over and over again, till we know them almost by heart. We've both had letters from Mother and Molly, and Big Joe's put his mark at the bottom of each one, his smudged thumbprint in ink with "Joe" written large beside it in heavily indented pencil. That makes us smile. I can see him writing it, nose to the paper, tongue between his teeth. Mother writes that they're turning most of the Big

House into a hospital for officers, and the Wolfwoman rules the roost up there more than ever. Molly says the Wolfwoman now wears a lady's wide-brimmed straw hat with a big white ostrich feather instead of her old black bonnet, and that she smiles all the time "like Lady Muck." Molly writes too, that she's missing me, and that she is well, except that she feels a little sick sometimes. She hopes the war will be over quickly and then we can all be together again. I can't read the rest, or her name, because Joe's finger has blotted everything else out.

They let us out of camp for an evening and we go into the nearest village, Poperinghe, "Pop" everyone seems to call it. Captain Wilkes tells us there's an *estaminet* there — that's a sort of pub he says, where you can drink the best beer outside England and eat the best egg and chips in the entire world. He's right. Pete, and Nipper, Little Les, Charlie and me stuff ourselves on egg and chips and beer. We're like camels filling up at an oasis that we've discovered by accident and may never find again.

There's a girl in the restaurant who smiles at me when she clears the plates away. She's the daughter of the owner, who is always very smartly dressed and very round and very merry, like a Father Christmas without the beard. It's difficult to believe she's his daughter, for in every way she's the opposite, wonderfully elf-like and delicate. Nipper notices her smiling at me and makes something dirty of it. She knows it and moves away. But I don't forget her smile, nor the egg and chips and the beer. Charlie and me drink to the Colonel and the Wolfwoman again and again, wishing them all the misfortune and misery and all the little monster children they so richly deserve, and then we stagger back to camp. I'm properly drunk for the first time in my life, and feel very proud of myself, until I lie down and my bead swirls and threatens to drag me down into some black abyss where I fear to go. I struggle to think straight, to picture the girl in the *estaminet* in Pop. But the more I think of her the more I see Molly.

The big guns bring me to my senses. We crawl out of our tent into the night. The sky is lit up all along the horizon. Whoever is underneath all that, friend or foe, is taking a terrible pounding. "That's Ypres," says the captain beside me in the darkness.

"Poor beggars," says someone else. "Glad we're not in Wipers tonight."

We go back to our tent, huddle under our blankets and thank God it's not us, but every one of us knows our time must come, and soon.

The next evening we go up into the line. There are no big guns tonight, but rifle fire and machine-gun fire crackle and rattle ahead of us, and flares go up, intermittently lighting the darkness. We know we are close now. It seems as if the road is taking us down into the earth itself, until it is a road no more, but rather a tunnel without a roof, a communications trench. We have to be silent now. Not a whisper, not a word. If the German machine gunners or mortars spot us, and there are places they can, then we're done for. So we stifle our curses as we slither and slide in the mud, holding on to one another to stop ourselves from falling. A line of soldiers passes us coming the other way, dark-eyed men, sullen and weary. No need for questions. No need for answers. The haunted, hunted look in their eyes tells it all.

We find our dugout at last, every one of us yearning only for sleep now. It has been a long, cold march. A mug of hot sweet tea and to lie down, it's all I want. But with Charlie, I'm posted to sentry duty. For the first time I look out through the wire over no-man's-land and towards the enemy trenches, less than two hundred yards from our front line, they tell us, but we can't see them, only the wire. The night is still now. A machine gun stutters and instantly I duck down. I needn't have bothered. It's one of ours. I'm overwhelmed by fear, numbed by it, and for the moment that fear banishes the wretched discomfort of my wet feet and frozen hands. I feel

Charlie there beside me. "Fine night for poaching, Tommo," he whispers. I can see his smile in the dark and my fear is gone at once.

It's just as the captain said it would be, quiet. Every day I wait for the Germans to shell us, and they don't. It seems they're too busy shelling Wipers further up the line to bother about us, and I can't say I'm sorry. I even begin to hope that they might have run out of shells. Every time I look through the periscope I expect to see the grey hordes coming at us across no-man's-land, but no one comes. I am almost disappointed. We hear occasional sniper fire, so there is no smoking in the trenches at night, "unless you want your head shot off," the captain says. Our artillery lobs a shell or two over into their trenches once in a while, and they do the same. Each one, theirs or ours — and ours sometimes drop short — comes as a surprise and terrifies me at first, terrifies all of us, but in time we become used to it and pay less attention.

Our trench and our dugouts have been left in a mess by the previous occupants, a company of Jocks from the Seaforths, so when we're not on stand-to at dawn, brewing up or sleeping, we're set to clearing up their mess. Captain Wilkes — or "Wilkie" as we call him now — is meticulous about tidiness and cleanliness, "because of the rats," he says. We find out soon enough he's right again. I am the first to find them. I am detailed to begin shoring up a dilapidated trench wall. I plunge my shovel in and open up an entire nest of them. They come pouring out, skittering away over my boots. I recoil in horror for a moment and then set about stamping them to death in the mud. I don't kill a single one, and we see them everywhere after that. Fortunately we have Little Les, our own professional rat-catcher, who is now called upon whenever a rat is spotted, whatever the time, day or night, he doesn't mind. He jokes that it makes him feel at home. He knows the ways of rats, and kills with a will each time, tossing their corpses up into no-man's-land with a flourish of triumph. After a while the rats seem to know they have met their match in Little Les and leave us be.

But our other daily curse, lice, we all have to deal with ourselves. Each of us has to burn off his own with a lighted cigarette end. They inhabit us wherever they can, the folds of our skin, the creases of our clothes. We long for a bath to drown the lot of them, but above all we long to be warm again and dry.

Our greatest scourge is neither rats nor fleas but the un-ending drenching rain, which runs like a stream along the bottom of our trench, turning it into nothing but a mud-filled ditch, a stinking gooey mud that seems to want to hold us and then suck us down and drown us. I have not had dry feet since I got here. I go to sleep wet. I wake up wet, and the cold soaks through my sodden clothes and into my aching bones. Only sleep brings any real relief, sleep and food. God, how we long for both. Wilkie moves among us at dawn on the firestep, a word here, a smile there. He keeps us going, keeps us up to the mark. If he has fear he never shows it, and if that is courage then we're beginning to catch it.

But we couldn't do without Charlie either. It's Charlie who keeps us together, breaks up our squabbles (which are many and frequent now that we are so closely confined together) and jollies each of us along when we get downhearted. He's become like a big brother to everyone. After Sergeant Hanley and the field punishment, and the way Charlie managed to smile through it all, there isn't a man in the company who doesn't look up to him. Being his real brother I could feel I live in his shadow, but I never have and I do not now. I live in his glow.

We have a few more miserable days in the line, all of us longing for the comforts of rest camp. But when we get there they keep us endlessly busy. We clean our kit, march up and down, turn out for inspections again and again, do our gas mask drill again, and then there are always more ditches and drains to dig to take away the incessant rain. But we do have letters from home, from Molly and Mother, and they have knitted woolen scarves and gloves and socks for us both. We have communal baths in great steaming vats in a barn down the road and, best of all, eggs and chips and beer at the *estaminet* in Pop. The beautiful girl with the doe eyes is there, but she does not always notice me, and when she doesn't I drink even more, to drown my sorrows.

The first snow of winter sees us back in the trenches. It freezes as it falls, hardening the mud — and that certainly is a blessing. Providing there is no wind we are no colder than we were before and can at least keep our feet dry. The guns have stayed relatively silent in our sector and we have had few casualties so far: one wounded by a sniper, two in hospital with pneumonia, and one with chronic trench foot — which affects us all. From what we hear and read we are in just about the luckiest sector we could be.

Word has come down from Headquarters, Wilkie says, that we must send out patrols to find out what regiments have come into the line opposite us and in what strength — though why we have to do that we do not know. There are spotter planes doing that almost every day. So most nights now, four or five of us are picked, and a patrol goes out into no-man's-land to find out what they can. More often than not they find out nothing. No one likes going, of course, but nobody's been hurt so far, and you get a double rum ration before you go, and everyone wants that.

My turn soon comes up as it was bound to. I'm not particularly worried. Charlie's going with me, and Nipper Martin, Little Les and Pete — "the whole skittle team," Charlie calls us. Wilkie's heading the patrol and we're glad of that. He tells us we have to achieve what the other patrols have not. We have to bring back one prisoner for questioning. They give us each a double rum ration, and I'm warmed instantly to the roots of my hair, to the toes of my feet.

"Stay close, Tommo," Charlie whispers, and then we are climbing out over the top, crawling on our bellies through the wire. We snake our way forward. We slither into a shell hole and lie doggo there for a while in case we've been heard. We can hear Fritz talking now, and laughing. There's the sound of a gramophone playing — I've heard all this before on lookout, but distantly. We're close now, very close, and I should be scared witless. Strangely, I find I'm not so much frightened as excited. Maybe it's the rum. I'm out poaching again, that's what it feels like. I'm tensed for danger. I'm ready for it, but not frightened.

It takes an eternity to cross no-man's-land. I begin to wonder if we'll ever find their trenches at all. Then we see their wire up ahead. We wriggle through a gap, and, still undetected, we drop down into their trench. It looks deserted, but we know it can't be. We can still hear the voices and the music. I notice the trench is much deeper than ours, wider too, and altogether more solidly constructed. I grip my rifle tighter and follow Charlie along the trench, bent double like everyone else. We're trying not to, but we're making too much noise. I can't understand why no one has heard us. Where are their sentries, for God's sake? Up ahead I can see Wilkie waving us on with his revolver. There is a flickering of light now coming from a dugout ahead, where the voices are, where the music is. From the sound of it there could be half a dozen men in there at least. We only need one prisoner. How are we going to manage half a dozen of them?

At that moment the light floods into the trench as the dugout curtain opens. A soldier comes out shrugging on his coat, the curtain closing behind him. He is alone, just what we are after. He doesn't seem to see us right away. Then he does. For a split second the Hun does nothing and neither do we. We just stand and look at one another. He could so easily have done what he should have done, just put up his hands and come with us. Instead he lets out a shriek and turns, blundering through the curtain back into the dugout. I don't know who threw the grenade in after him, but there is a blast that throws me back against the trench wall. I sit there stunned.

There is screaming and firing from inside the dugout, then silence. The music has stopped.

By the time I get in there Little Les is lying on his side shot through the head, his eyes staring at me. He looks so surprised. Several Germans are sprawled across their dugout, all still, all dead — except one. He stands there naked, blood-spattered and shaking. I too, am shaking. He has his hands in the air and is whimpering. Wilkie throws a coat over him and Pete bundles him out of the dugout. Frantic now to get back we scrabble our way up out of the trench, the Hun still whimpering. He is beside himself with terror. Pete is shouting at him to stop, but he's only making it worse. We follow the captain through the German wire and run.

For a while I think we have got away with it, but then a flare goes up and we are caught suddenly in broad daylight. I hurl myself to the ground and bury my face in the snow. Their flares last so much longer than ours, shine so much brighter. I know we're in for it. I press myself into the ground, eyes closed. I'm praying and thinking of Molly. If I'm going to die I want her to be my last thought. But she's not. Instead I'm saying sorry to Father for what I did, that I didn't mean to do it. A machine gun opens up behind us and then rifles fire. There is nowhere to hide, so we pretend to be dead. We wait till the light dies and the night is suddenly black again. Wilkie gets us to our feet and we go on, running, stumbling, until more lights go up, and the machine gunners start up again. We dive into a crater and roll down crashing through the ice into the watery bottom. Then the shelling starts. It seems as if we have woken up the entire German army. I cower in the stinking water with the German and Charlie, the three of us clinging together, heads buried in one another as the shells fall all about us. Our own guns are answering now but it is little comfort to us. Charlie and I drag the Hun prisoner out of the water. Either he is talking to himself or he's saying a prayer, it's difficult to tell.

Then we see Wilkie lying higher up the slope, too close to the lip of the crater. When Charlie calls out to him he doesn't reply. Charlie goes to him and turns him over. "It's my legs," I hear the captain whisper. "I can't seem to move my legs." He's too exposed up there, so Charlie drags him back down as gently as he can. We try to make him comfortable. The Hun keeps praying out loud. I'm quite sure he's praying now. "*Du lieber Gott,*" I hear. They call God by the same name. Pete and Nipper are crawling over towards us from the far side of the crater. We are together at least. The ground shudders, and with every impact we are bombarded by showers of mud and stone and snow. But the sound I hate and fear most is not the sound of the explosion — by then it's done and over with, and you're either dead or not. No, it's the whistle and whine and shriek of the shells as they come over. It's the not knowing where they will land, whether this one is for you.

Then, as suddenly as the barrage begins, it stops. There is silence. Darkness hides us again. Smoke drifts over us and down into our hole, filling our nostrils with the stench of cordite. We stifle our coughing. The Hun has stopped his praying, and is lying curled up in his overcoat, his hands over his ears. He's rocking like a child, like Big Joe.

"I won't make it," Wilkie says to Charlie. "I'm leaving it to you to get them all back, Peaceful, and the prisoner. Go on now."

"No sir," Charlie replies. "If one goes we all go. Isn't that right, lads?"

That's how it happened. Under cover of an early-morning mist we made it back to our trenches, Charlie carrying Wilkie on his back the whole way, until the stretcher bearers came for him in the trench. As they lifted him, Wilkie caught Charlie by the hand and held it. "Come and see me in hospital, Peaceful," he said. "That's an order." And Charlie promised he would.

We had a brew up with our prisoner in the dugout before they came for him. He smoked a cigarette Pete had given him. He'd stopped shaking now, but his eyes still held their fear. We had nothing to say to one another until the moment he got up to leave. *"Danke,"* he said. *"Danke sehr."*

"Funny that," Nipper said when he'd gone. "Seeing him standing there with not a stitch on. Take off our uniforms and you can hardly tell the difference, can you? Not a bad bloke, for a Fritz that is."

That night I didn't think, as I should have done, of Little Les lying out there in the German dugout, with a hole in his head. I thought of the Hun prisoner we'd brought back. I didn't even know his name, yet, after that night cowering in the shell hole with him, I felt somehow I knew him better than I'd ever known Little Les.

We are back at last at rest camp, most of us anyway. We soon find out which hospital Wilkie is in, and we go to see him as Charlie had promised. It's a big chateau of a place, with ambulances coming and going, and crisp-looking nurses bustling everywhere. "Who are you?" asks the orderly at the desk.

"Peaceful," says Charlie smiling — he loves playing this joke. "Both of us are Peaceful."

The orderly does not look amused, but he seems to have been expecting us. "Which of you is Charlie Peaceful?"

"I am," said Charlie.

"Captain Wilkes said you would come." The orderly is

reaching into the desk drawer. He takes out a watch. "He left this for you," he says, and Charlie takes the watch.

"Where is he?" Charlie asks. "Can we see him?"

"Back in Blighty by now. Left yesterday. In a bad way. Nothing more we could do for him here, I'm afraid."

As we walk down the steps of the hospital Charlie is putting the watch on his wrist.

"Does it work?" I ask.

"Course it does," he says. He shows it to me on his wrist. "What d'you think?"

"Nice," I reply.

"It's not just nice, Tommo," Charlie says. "It's wonderful, that's what it is. Ruddy wonderful. Tell you what — if anything happens to me it's yours, all right?"

TWENTY-FIVE PAST THREE

The mouse is here again. He keeps stopping and looking up at me. He's wondering if he should run away, whether I'm friend or foe. *"Wee, sleekit, caw'rin tim'rous beastie."* I don't know what half the words mean, but I still know the poem. Back at school Miss McAllister made us stand up and recite it on Burns Day. She said it was good for us to have at least one great Scottish poem in our heads forever. This wee beastie is tim'rous all right, but he's not Scottish, he's a Belgian mouse. I recite the poem to him all the same. He seems to understand because he listens politely. I do it in Miss

McAllister's Scottish accent. I'm almost word perfect; I think Miss McAllister would have been proud of me. But the moment I finish he's gone, and I'm alone once more.

Earlier they came and asked if I wanted someone to stay with me through the night, and I said no. I even sent the padre away. They asked if there was anything I wanted, anything they could do to help, and I said there was nothing. Now I long to have them all here, the padre too. We could have had singsongs. They could have brought me egg and chips. We could have drunk ourselves silly and I could be numb with it by now. But all I've had for company is a mouse, a vanishing Belgian mouse.

The next time they sent us up into the line it wasn't back to our "quiet" sector, it was into the Wipers salient itself. For months now Fritz had been pounding away at Wipers, trying everything he could to batter it into submission. Time and again he'd almost broken through into the town and had only been driven back at the last moment. But the salient around the town was shrinking all the time. From the talk in the *estaminet* in Pop and from the almost constant bombardment a few miles to the east of us, we all knew how bad it must be in there. Everyone knew they had us surrounded and overlooked on three sides, so that they could chuck all they wanted into our trenches, and there was nothing much we could do about it, except grin and bear it.

Our new company commander, Lieutenant Buckland, told us how things were, how if we gave way then Wipers would be lost, and that Wipers must not be lost. He didn't say why it mustn't be lost, but then he wasn't Wilkie. We all felt the loss of Wilkie very keenly. Without him we were like sheep without a shepherd. Lieutenant Buckland was doing his best, but he was straight out from England. He might have been very properly spoken, but he knew even less about fighting this war than we did. Nipper said he was just a young pipsqueak, and that he belonged back at school. And it was true, he seemed younger than any of us, even me.

As we marched through Wipers that evening I wondered why it was worth fighting for at all. So far as I could see there was no town left, nothing you could call a town anyway. Rubble and ruin, that's all the place was, more dogs and cats than townspeople. We saw two horses lying dead and mangled in the street, as we passed by what was left of the town hall; and everywhere there were soldiers and guns and ambulances on the move, and hurrying. They were not shelling the town as we came through, but I was as terrified then as I ever had been. I could not get those horses and their terrible wounds out of my head. The sight of them haunted me, haunted all of us, I think. None of us sang. None of us talked. I longed only to reach the sanctuary of our new trenches, to crawl into the deepest dugout I could find and hide.

But when we got there the trenches were a bitter disappointment to us. Wilkie would have been appalled at the state of them. In places they were little more than shallow dilapidated ditches affording us precious little protection, and the mud here was even deeper than before. There was a sickly-sweet stench about the place that had to be more than stagnant mud and water. I knew well enough what it was, we all did, but no one dared speak of it. Word came back that from now on we should keep our heads down because here was where we could be most easily spotted by their snipers. But there was at least some consolation when we reached the dugout. It was the best we'd ever had, deep and warm and dry. I could not sleep though. I lay there that night, knowing how a hunted fox must feel lying low in his lair with the hounds waiting for him outside.

I am on stand-to the next morning, locked inside my gas mask in a world of my own, listening to myself breathing. The mist rises over no-man's-land. I see in front of me a blasted wasteland. No vestige of fields or trees here, not a blade of grass — simply a land of mud and craters. I see unnatural humps scattered over there beyond our wire. They are the unburied, some in field-grey uniforms and some in khaki. There is one lying in the wire with his arm stretched heavenwards, his hand pointing. He is one of ours, or was. I look up where he is pointing. There are birds up there, and they are singing. I see a beady-eyed blackbird singing to the world from his barbed-wire perch. He has no tree to sing from.

The pipsqueak of a lieutenant says, "Keep your eyes peeled, lads. Keep your wits about you." He's always doing that, always telling us to do things we're already doing. But nothing moves out there in no-man's-land but the crows. It is a dead man's land.

We're back down in the dugout after stand-to, brewing up when the bombardment starts. It doesn't stop for two whole days. They are the longest two days of my life. I cower there, we all do, each of us alone in our own private misery. We cannot talk for the din. There can be little sleep. When I do sleep I see the hand pointing skywards, and it is Father's hand, and I wake shaking. Nipper Martin has got the shakes too, and Pete tries to calm him but he can't. I cry like a baby sometimes and not even Charlie can comfort me. We want nothing more than for it to stop, for the earth to be still again, for there to be quiet. I know that when it's over they'll be coming for us, that I'll have to be ready for them, for the gas maybe, or the flame-thrower, or the grenades, or the bayonets. But I don't mind how they come. Let them come. I just want this to stop. I just want it to be over.

When at last it does we are ordered out on to the firestep, gas masks on, bayonets fixed, eyes straining through the smoke that drifts across in front of us. Then out of the smoke we see them come, their bayonets glinting, one or two at first, but then hundreds, thousands. Charlie's there beside me.

"You'll be all right, Tommo," he says. "You'll be fine."

He knows my thoughts. He sees my terror. He knows I want to run.

"Just do what I do, right? And stay by me."

I stay and I do not run, only because of Charlie. The firing starts all along the line, machine guns and rifle fire, shelling, and I'm firing too. I'm not aiming, just firing, firing, loading and firing again. And still they do not stop. For a few moments it seems as if bullets do not touch them. They come on towards us unscathed, an army of invincible grey ghosts. Only when they begin to crumple and cry out and fall do I begin to believe they are mortal. And they are brave too. They do not falter. No matter how many are cut down, those that are left keep coming. I can see their wild eyes as they reach our wire. It is the wire that stops them. Somehow enough of it has survived the bombardment. Only a few of them find the gaps, and they are shot down before they ever reach our trenches. Those that are left, and there are not many now, have turned and are stumbling back, some throwing away their rifles. I feel a surge of triumph welling inside me, not because we have won, but because I have stood with the others. I have not run.

"Y'ain't a coward, are you?"

No, old woman, I am not, I am not.

Then the whistle goes, and I am up with the others and after them. We pour through the gap in the wire. They lie here so thick on the ground it is hard not to step on them. I have no pity for them, but no hatred either. They came to kill us, and we killed them. I look up. They are running from us as we go forward. We fire at will now, picking them off. We are across no-man's-land before we know it. We find a way through their wire and leap down into their frontline trenches. I am a hunter seeking out my quarry, a quarry I will kill, but my quarry has gone. The trench is deserted.

Lieutenant Buckland is up on the parapet above us, screaming at us to follow him, that we've got them on the run. I follow. We all follow. He is not so much of a pipsqueak as we all thought. Everywhere I look, to my right, to my left, as far as I can see, we are advancing and I am a part of it and

I feel suddenly exhilarated. But in front of us the enemy seems to have vanished, I am unsure what to do now. I look all around for Charlie, and cannot see him anywhere. That's when the first shell comes screaming over. I throw myself down, flatten myself into the mud, as it explodes close behind me, deafening me instantly. After a while I force myself to lift up my head and look. Ahead of me I see us advancing still, and everywhere in front of us the flash of rifle fire, the spitting flame of machine guns. For a moment I think I am dead already. All is soundless, all is unreal. A silent storm of shelling rages about me. Before my eyes we are scythed down, blown apart, obliterated. I see men crying out but I hear nothing. It is as if I am not there, as if this horror cannot touch me.

They are stumbling back towards me now. I can't see Charlie among them. The lieutenant grabs me and hauls me to my feet. He's shouting at me, then turning me and pushing me back towards our trenches. I am trying to run with the others, trying to keep with them. But my legs are leaden and will not let me run. The lieutenant stays with me, urging me on, urging us all on. He is a good man. He's right there alongside me when he's hit. He drops to his knees and dies looking up at me. I see the light fade in his eyes. I watch him fall forward on his face. I do not know how I manage to get back after that, but I do, I find myself curled up in the dugout, and the dugout is half-empty. Charlie is not there. He has not come back.

At least I can hear again now, even if it is mostly the ringing in my head. Pete has news of Charlie. He says he's sure he saw him on the way back from the German trenches, hobbling, using his rifle as a stick, but all right. That gives me some fragile hope, but it is hope that ebbs away as the hours pass. As I lie there I relive each and every horror. I see the puzzled look on the lieutenant's face as he kneels there, trying to speak to me. I see a thousand silent screams. To drive these visions away I tell myself all manner of reassuring tales about Charlie: how Charlie must be out there in some crater, only waiting for the clouds to cover the moon before he crawls back; how he's got himself lost and has landed up somewhere down the line with another regiment and will find his way back to us in the morning — it happens all the time. My mind races and will not let me rest. There is no shelling to interrupt my thoughts. Outside the world has fallen silent. Both armies lie exhausted in their trenches and bleeding to death.

By stand-to the next morning I knew for sure that Charlie would not be coming back, that all my stories had been just that, stories. Pete and Nipper and the others had tried to convince me that he might still be alive. But I knew he was not. I was not grieving. I was numb inside, as void of all feeling as the hands that clutched my rifle. I looked out over no-man's-land where Charlie had died. They lay as if they'd been heaped against the wire by the wind, and Charlie, I knew, was one of them. I wondered what I would write to Molly and Mother. I could hear Mother's voice in my head, hear her telling Big Joe how Charlie would not be coming back, how he had gone to Heaven to be with Father and Bertha. Big Joe would be sad. He would rock. He would hum *Oranges and Lemons* mournfully up his tree. But after a few days his faith would comfort him. He would believe absolutely that Charlie was up there in the blue of Heaven, high above the church tower somewhere. I envied him that. I could no longer even pretend to myself that I believed in a merciful god, nor in a heaven, not any more, not after I had seen what men could do to one another. I could believe only in the hell I was living in, a hell on earth, and it was man-made, not God-made.

That night, like a man sleepwalking, I got up to take my turn on sentry duty. The sky was filled with stars. Molly knew the stars well — the Plow, the Milky Way, the Pole Star — she'd often tried to teach me them all when we were out poaching. I tried to remember, tried to identify them in amongst the millions, and failed. As I was looking up in wonder at the immensity and beauty of it all, I found myself almost believing in Heaven again. I picked one bright star in the west to be Charlie, and another next to him. That was Father. They were together looking down on me. I wished then I had told Charlie about how Father had died, for there would be no secrets between us now. I shouldn't have kept it from him. So, unspeaking, I told him then, saw him glisten and wink at me, and knew he had understood and did not blame me. Then I heard Charlie's voice in my head. "Don't go all dreamy on lookout, Tommo," he was saying. "You'll fall asleep. You can get shot for that." I widened my eyes, blinked them hard, and took in a deep gulp of cold air to wake me up.

Only moments later I saw something move out beyond the wire. I listened. There was still a ringing in my ears, so I couldn't be sure of it, but I thought I could hear someone, a voice, and a voice that was not inside my head. It was a whisper. "Hey! Anyone there? It's me, Charlie Peaceful. D Company. I'm coming in. Don't shoot." Perhaps I was already asleep and deep in a wonderful dream I wanted to be true. But the voice came again, louder this time. "What's the matter with you lot? Are you all fast asleep or what? It's Charlie, Charlie Peaceful."

From under the wire a dark shape shifted and moved towards me. Not a dream, not one of my make-believe stories. It was Charlie. I could see his face now and he could see mine. "Tommo, you dozy beggar, you. Give us a hand, will you?" I grabbed him and tumbled him down into the trench. "Am I glad to see you!" he said. We hugged one another then. I don't think we ever had before. I cried, and tried unsuccessfully to hide it, until I felt him crying too.

"What happened?" I asked.

"They shot me in the foot, can you believe it? Shot right through my boot. I bled like a pig. I was on my way back and I passed out in some shell hole. Then by the time I woke up all you lot had gone off and left me. I had to stay put till nightfall. Seems like I've been crawling all bloody night."

"Does it hurt?"

"I can't feel a thing," Charlie said. "But then, I can't feel the other foot either — I'm frozen stiff. Don't you worry, Tommo. I'll be right as rain."

They stretchered him to hospital that night, and I did not see him again until they pulled us out of the line a few days later. Pete and I went to see him as soon as we could. He was sitting up in his bed and grinning all over his face. "It's good in here," he said. "You want to try it sometime. Three decent meals a day, nurses, no mud, and a nice long way from Mister Fritz."

"How's the foot?" I asked him.

"Foot? What foot?" He patted his leg. "That's not a foot,

Tommo. That's my ticket home. Some nice, kind Mister Fritz gave me the best present he could, a ticket home to Blighty. They're sending me to a hospital back home. It's a bit infected. Lots of bones broken, they said. It'll mend, but it'll take an operation, and then I've got to rest it up. So they're packing me off tomorrow."

I knew I should be pleased for him, and I wanted to be, but I just could not bring myself to think that way. All I could think was that we'd come to this war together. We'd stuck together through thick and thin, and now he was breaking the bond between us, and deserting me. Worst of all he was going home without me, and he was so unashamedly happy about it.

"I'll give them your best, Tommo," he said. "Pete'll keep an eye on you for me. You'll look after him, won't you Pete?"

"I don't need looking after," I snapped.

But Charlie either hadn't heard me or he ignored me. "And you make sure he behaves, Pete. That girl in the *estaminet* in Pop, she's got her eye on him. She'll eat him alive." They laughed at my embarrassment, and I could not disguise my hurt and discomfort. "Hey, Tommo." Charlie put his hand on my arm. "I'll be back before you know it." And he was serious now, for the first time. "Promise," he said.

"You'll be seeing Molly, then, and Mother?" I asked.

"Just let them try and stop me," he said. "I'll wangle a bit of leave. Or maybe they'll come and see me in hospital. With a bit of luck I could get to see the baby. Less than a month to go now, Tommo, and I'll be a father. You'll be an uncle too. Think of that."

But the evening after Charlie had left for Blighty I wasn't thinking of that at all. I was in the *estaminet* in Pop drowning my anger in beer. And it *was* anger I was drowning, not just sorrows: anger at Charlie for abandoning me, anger that he was to see Molly and home, and that I was not. In my befuddled state I even thought of deserting, of going after him. I'd make my way to the Channel and find a boat. I'd get home somehow.

I looked around me. There must have been a hundred or more soldiers in the place that evening, Pete and Nipper Martin, and some of the others among them, but I felt completely alone. They were laughing and I could not laugh. They were singing and I could not sing. I couldn't even eat my egg and chips. It was stiflingly hot in there and the air was thick with cigarette smoke. I could hardly breathe. I went outside to get some air. That brought me very quickly to my senses, and I gave up at once all idea of deserting. I would go back to camp instead. It was the easier choice — you can get shot for desertion.

"Tommy?"

It was her, the girl from the *estaminet.* She was carrying out a crate of wine bottles.

"You are ill?" she asked me.

Tongue tied, I shook my head. We stood for some moments listening to the thunder of the guns as a heavy barrage opened up over Wipers, the sky lit up over the town like an angry sunset. Flares rose and hovered and fell over the front line.

"It is beautiful," she said. "How can it be beautiful?"

I wanted to speak, but I did not trust myself to do so. I felt suddenly overwhelmed by tears, by longing for home and for Molly.

"How old?" she asked.

"Sixteen," I muttered.

"Like me," she said. I found her looking at me more closely. "I have seen you before, I think?" I nodded. "I will see you again perhaps?"

"Yes," I said. Then she was gone and I was alone again in the night. I was calmer now, more at peace with myself and stronger too. Walking back to camp I made up my mind. We were being sent away for training the next day, but as soon as I came back, I would go straight to Pop, to the *estaminet,* and when the girl brought me my egg and chips I would be brave — I would ask her her name.

Two weeks later I was back, and that's just what I did. "Anna," she told me. And she tinkled with laughter when I told her my name was Tommo. "It's true then," she said. "Every English soldier is called Tommy."

"I'm not Tommy, I'm Tommo," I replied.

"It's the same," she laughed. "But you're different, different from the others, I think."

When she heard I had worked on a farm, and with horses, she took me into the stable and showed me her father's carthorse. He was massive and magnificent. Our hands met as we patted him. She kissed me then, brushed my cheek with her lips. I left her and walked back along the gusty road to camp under the high riding moon, singing *Oranges and Lemons* at the top of my voice.

Pete greeted me in the tent with a scowl. "You won't be so ruddy happy, Tommo, when you hear what I've got to tell you."

"What?" I asked.

"Our new sergeant. It's only Horrible-bleeding-Hanley from Etaples."

From then on, every waking hour of every day, Hanley was at us. We'd been mollycoddled, he said. We were sloppy soldiers and he was going to lick us back into shape. And we weren't allowed out of camp until he was satisfied. And of course he was never satisfied. So I couldn't get out of camp to see Anna again. By the time we went back up into the line, Hanley snapping at our heels, his voice had become a vicious bark inside each of our heads. Every one of us hated him like poison, a great deal more than we had ever hated Fritz.

NEARLY FOUR
O'CLOCK

There is the beginning of day in the night sky, not yet the pale light of dawn, but night is certainly losing its darkness. A cockerel sounds his morning call, and tells me what I already know but do not want to believe, that morning will break, and soon.

Morning at home used to be walking with Charlie to school, wading through piles of autumn leaves and stamping the ice in the puddles, or the three of us coming up through the woods after a night's poaching on the Colonel's river, and crouching down to watch a badger that didn't know we were there. Morning here has always been to wake with the same dread in the pit of my stomach, knowing that I will have to look death in the face again, that up to now it may have been someone else's death, but that today it could be mine, that this may be my last sunrise, my last day on earth.

All that is different about this morning is that I know whose death it will be and how it will happen.

Looking at it that way it seems not so bad. Look at it that way, Tommo. Look at it that way.

I always imagined I'd be lost without Charlie at my side, and the truth is that I might have been had it not been for the new batch of recruits that joined us straight from home. And how we needed them. Almost half of us were missing by this time, killed or wounded or sick. Those of us that were left were to them battle-hardened soldiers, old lags who had seen it all, and therefore to be admired, respected, and even a little feared, it seemed. Young though I still felt, I don't think I looked it, not any more. Pete and Nipper Martin and I were old soldiers now, and we behaved like it, alternately reassuring the new recruits or terrifying them with our stories, befriending them or teasing them. I think we rather played up to the role they gave us and we revelled in it too, particularly Pete, who was more inventive with his stories than Nipper and me. All this gave me less time to dwell on my own fears. I was far too busy pretending I was someone else.

For some time, life was about as quiet as it could get in the front line. We and Fritz did little more than irritate each other with occasional whizzbangs and night patrols, and in the close confinement of the dugout and the trenches, even Sergeant Hanley could do little to make our lives any more of a misery than they already were, though he still did his very best, with an endless succession of inspections and consequent punishments. But for days on end the guns stayed silent, the spring sun shone, warming our backs and drying out the mud. And best of all, we went to bed dry — a rare treat, a miraculous treat. Yes, the rats were still there and the lice loved us as much as ever, but this was a picnic compared to all we'd been through before.

By now I think the new recruits were all beginning to think that we old lags had been exaggerating with some of our harsher tales of trench warfare. Boredom and Sergeant Hanley seemed to them to be the worst they had had to endure so far. And it was certainly true, particularly in Pete's case, that we had laid it on a bit thick. But Pete, like the rest of us, had, for the most part anyway, told them stories that had at least some connection with the truth. None of us, not even

Pete, could have imagined or invented what would happen to us on the quietest of May mornings, when we were least expecting it.

Stand-to on the firestep at dawn had been normal, by now a mere routine, and an annoying one too. Attacks came mostly at dawn, we knew that, but after all this time we expected nothing to happen, and nothing had happened, not for a long while now. We were lulled by the blue skies perhaps, or by sheer boredom. Fritz seemed to have gone to sleep on us and as far as we were concerned that suited us fine. We thought we could go to sleep too. The awakening came suddenly. I was in the dugout, and I was just beginning a letter home.

I am writing to Mother — I haven't written for a while and am feeling guilty about it. My pencil keeps breaking and I am sharpening it again. Everyone else is lying asleep in the sun or is sitting about smoking and chatting. Nipper Martin is cleaning his rifle again. He's always very particular about that.

"Gas! Gas!"

The cry goes up and is echoed all along the trench. For a moment we are frozen with panic. We have trained for this time and again, but nonetheless we fumble clumsily, feverishly with our gas masks.

"Fix bayonets!" Hanley's yelling while we're still trying frantically to pull on our gas masks. We grab our rifles and fix bayonets. We're on the firestep looking out into no-man's-land, and we see it rolling towards us, this dreaded killer cloud we have heard so much about but have never seen for ourselves until now. Its deadly tendrils are searching ahead, feeling their way forward in long yellow wisps, scenting me, searching for me. Then finding me out, the gas turns and drifts straight for me. I'm shouting inside my gas mask. "Christ! Christ!" Still the gas comes on, wafting over our wire, through our wire, swallowing everything in its path.

I hear again in my head the instructor's voice, see him shouting at me through his mask when we went out on our last exercise. "You're panicking in there, Peaceful. A gas mask is like God, son. It'll work bloody miracles for you, but you've got to believe in it." But I don't believe in it! I don't believe in miracles.

The gas is only feet away now. In a moment it will be on me, around me, in me. I crouch down hiding my face between my knees, hands over my helmet, praying it will float over my head, over the top of the trench and seek out someone else. But it does not. It's all around me. I tell myself I will not breathe, I must not breathe. Through a yellow mist I see the trench filling up with it. It drifts into the dugouts, snaking into every nook and cranny, looking for me. It wants to seek us all out, to kill us all, every one of us. Still I do not breathe. I see men running, staggering, falling. I hear Pete shouting out for me. Then he's grabbing me and we run. I have to breathe now. I can't run without breathing. Half-blinded by my mask I trip and fall, crashing my head against the trench wall, knocking myself half-senseless. My gas mask has come off. I pull it down, but I have breathed in and know already it's too late. My eyes are stinging. My lungs are burning. I am coughing, retching, choking. I don't care where I'm running so long as it is away from the gas. At last I'm in the reserve trench and it is clear of gas. I'm out of it. I wrench off my mask, gasping for good air. Then I am on my hands and knees, vomiting violently. When at last the worst is over I look up through blurred and weeping eyes. A Hun in a gas mask is standing over me, his rifle aimed at my head. I have no rifle. It is the end. I brace myself, but he does not fire. He lowers his rifle slowly. "Go boy," he says, waving me away with his rifle. "Go. Tommy, go."

So by the whim of some kind and unknown Fritz I survived and escaped. Later, back at our field hospital I heard that we had counterattacked, and had driven the Germans back and retaken our frontline trenches but, from what I could see all around me, it was at a terrible cost. I lined up with the rest of the walking wounded to see the doctor. He washed out my eyes, examined them, and listened to my chest. Despite all my coughing he pronounced me fit. "You're lucky. You can only have got a whiff of it," he said.

As I walked away I passed the others, those that had not been as lucky. They were lying stretched out in the sun, many of them faces I knew, and would never see again; friends I had lived with, joked with, played cards with, fought with. I looked for Pete amongst them. He was not there. But Nipper Martin was, the last body I came to. He lay so still. There was a green grasshopper on his trousers. When I got back to rest camp that evening I found Pete alone in the tent. He looked up at me, wide-eyed, as if he had seen a ghost. When I told him about Nipper Martin he was as near to tears as I'd ever seen him. We exchanged our escape stories over a mug of hot sweet tea.

When the gas attack came, Pete had run like me, like most of us, but with some of the others he had then regrouped in the reserve trench, had been part of the counterattack. "We're still here, Tommo, we're alive," he said. "And that's all that matters I suppose. Unfortunately, so is Horrible-bloody-Hanley. But at least I've got some good news for you." He waved a couple of letters at me. "You've got two of them, you lucky devil. No one back home writes to me. Hardly surprising I suppose, because they can't write, can they? Well, my sister can, but we don't speak, not any more. Tell you what, Tommo, you can read yours out to me and then I can pretend they're written to me as well, can't I? Go on, Tommo. I'm listening." He lay back, put his hands under his head and closed his eyes. He didn't leave me much choice.

I have them with me now, my very last letters from home. I tried to keep all the others, but some got lost and others were so often soaked through that they became unreadable and I threw them away. But these I've looked after with the greatest of care because everyone I love is in them. I keep them in waxed paper in my pocket, close to my heart. I've read them over and over again, and each time I can hear their voices in the words, see their faces in the writing. I'll read them aloud again now, just as I read them to Pete that first time in the tent. I'll read Mother's letter first because I read it first then.

My dear Son,

I hope this letter finds you in good health. I have such good news to tell you. Last Monday, in the early morning, Molly gave birth to a little boy. As you can imagine we are all delighted at the happy event. You can imagine also our surprise and joy when I answered a knock on the door less than a week later to find your brother Charlie standing in the porch. He looks thinner than I remember him and much older too. I do not think he has been eating enough and have told him he must do so in future. He says that in spite of everything we read in the papers here you have been having a fine time together over in Belgium. Everyone I meet in the village asks how you are, even your great-aunt. She was the first to come to see the baby. She said that although he was handsome she thought he had rather pointed ears, which is untrue of course, and upset Molly greatly. Why does she always say such hurtful things? As for the Colonel, if we are to believe all he says, he could win this war all by himself. Your father was so right about him.

Much has changed in the village, and none of it for the better. More of our young men go to join up all the time. There are scarcely enough men left to work the land. Hedges go untrimmed and many fields lie fallow. Sad to say Fred and Margaret Parsons had news only last month that Jimmy will not be coming home. It seems he died of his wounds in France.

But Charlie's short visit and the birth of the baby have cheered us all. Charlie tells us that very soon there will be

another big push and then the war will be won and over
with. We pray he is right. Dear Son, even with Charlie
home, with Big Joe and Molly and the new baby, this lit-
tle house seems empty because you are not with us. Come
home safe and soon.

Your loving mother

And Big Joe's inky thumbprint was smeared along the bottom of the page as usual, with his name beside it in huge spidery lettering.

"So that's what we're having, is it?" said Pete suddenly and angrily. "A fine time. Why does he tell them that? Why doesn't he say what it's really like out here, what a hopeless bloody mess it all is, how there's good men, thousands of them, dying for nothing — for nothing! I'll tell them. Give me half a chance and I'll tell them. Saying things like that, Charlie should be ashamed of himself. Those men who died today, were they having a fine time? Were they?" I'd never seen Pete this angry before. He was always the joker, the wag, always playing the fool. He rolled over on his side with his back to me and didn't speak again.

So I read the next letter to myself. It was from Charlie, mostly anyway. Unlike Mother he'd made lots of mistakes and crossings out, so his letter was much harder to read.

Dear Private Peaceful,

I am home again as you can see, Tommo. Better late than never as they say. I am the proud father, and you are the proud uncle, of the finest looking little fellow you ever saw. I wish you could see him. But you will, and soon I hope. Molly tells me he is even more handsome than his father, which I'm very sure is not true. Big Joe sits over him while he sleeps, like he used to do with Bertha. He worries I shall go off again soon, which of course I shall. He does not understand — how could he? — where we have been or what we have been doing. And I'd rather not tell him. I'd rather not tell anyone.

After I came out of hospital I managed to wangle only three days' leave, of which I now have only one day left. I shall make the best of it. Lastly, you should know that we have all decided the little fellow will be called Tommo. Each time we say his name it makes me think you are here with us, as we all wish you were. Molly has said that she wants to write a few words also, so I shall end now. Chin up.

Your brother Charlie, or the other Private Peaceful

Dear Tommo,

I write to say that I have told little Tommo all about his brave uncle, about how one day when this dreadful war is over, we shall all be together again. He has your blue eyes, Charlie's dark hair and Big Joe's great grin. Because of all this I love him more than I can say.

Your Molly

These two letters I kept by me and read and re-read till I knew them almost by heart. They kept me going during the days ahead. I took from them the hope of Charlie's return, and the strength I needed to stop myself from going mad.

We might have thought, we certainly hoped, that Sergeant Hanley would let up on us now and let us rest before going back up into the line. But we were to discover what we should have known already, that this wasn't in his nature. He said we had shamed the regiment, that we had behaved like a bunch of cowards when the gas attack came, that if it was the last thing he did he would put backbone into us. So Hanley kept us at it morning, noon and night, day in, day out. Inspections, training, drilling, exercising, more inspections. He drove us mercilessly, drove us all to despair and exhaustion. Caught sleeping one night at his post, Ben Guy, the innkeeper's son from Exbourne, one of the new recruits, was subjected, as Charlie had been before him, to Field Punishment Number One. For day after day he was strapped there on the gun wheel in all weathers. As with Charlie at Etaples, we were forbidden even to speak to him or take him water.

These were the darkest days we had ever lived through. Sergeant Hanley had done what all the bloody attrition in the trenches had never done. He had taken away our spirit, and drained the last of our strength, destroyed our hope. More than once as I lay there in my tent at night I thought of deserting, or running to Anna in Pop and asking her to hide me, to help me find a way back to England. But when morning came, even my courage to be a coward had evaporated. I stayed each time because I was too cowardly to go, because I couldn't abandon Pete and the others, and not be there when Charlie got back. And I stayed too, because Molly had said I was brave and had named little Tommo after me. I couldn't shame her. I couldn't shame him.

Much to our surprise we were granted one night of freedom before we were to be sent off up into the line again, and we all headed straight into Pop, to the *estaminet*. Most of us were going for the beer and food, and I longed for all that as well, but as we walked into town I realized I had Anna on my mind a lot more than eggs and chips. But Anna did not bring us our beers. Another girl did, a girl none of us had seen before. I looked around me, but I could not see Anna serving at any of the other tables either. When the girl brought us our eggs and chips, I asked her where Anna was. She just shrugged as if she didn't understand, but there was something about her that told me she did understand, that she did know but would not tell me. Thanks to Pete and Charlie, my liking for Anna had not been a secret in the company for some time now, and now everyone was teasing me mercilessly as I looked around for her. Tiring of it, I left their mocking laughter behind me and went outside to look for her.

I looked first in the stable, where she'd taken me before, but it was empty. I walked down the darkening farm track past the henhouses to see if the horse might be out in the field, and Anna there with him. There were a couple of bleating tethered goats, but I could see no horse, and no Anna. Only then did I think of going back and knocking on the back door. I screwed my courage up. I had to knock loudly to be heard because of all the noise coming from the *estaminet*. The door opened slowly, and there was her father, not dapper and smiling as I'd always known him, but in his braces and shirt, unshaven and dishevelled. He had a bottle in his hand and his face was heavy with drink. He was not pleased to see me.

"Anna?" I asked. "Is Anna in?"

"No," he replied. "Anna isn't in. Anna will never be in again. Anna is dead. You hear this, Tommy? You come here and you fight your war in my place. Why? Tell me this. Why?"

"What happened?" I asked him.

"What happened? I tell you what happened. Two days ago I send Anna to fetch the eggs. She is driving the cart home along the road and a shell comes, a big Boche shell. Only one, but one is enough. I bury her today. So if you want to see my Anna, Tommy, then go to the graveyard. Then you can go to Hell, all of you, British, German, French, you think I care? And you can take your war to Hell with you, they will like it there. Leave me alone, Tommy, leave me alone."

The door was slammed shut in my face.

There were several recently dug graves in the churchyard, but I found only one that was freshly dug and covered with fresh flowers. I had known Anna only from a few laughing words, from the light in her eyes, a touch of hands and a fleeting kiss, but I felt an ache inside me such as I had not felt since I was a child, since my father's death. I looked up at the church steeple, a dark arrow pointing at the moon and beyond, and tried with all my heart and mind to believe she was up there somewhere in that vast expanse of infinity, up there in Sunday-school Heaven, in Big Joe's happy Heaven. I couldn't bring myself to think it. I knew she was lying in the cold earth at my feet. I knelt down and kissed the earth, then left her there. The moon sailed above me, following behind me, through the trees, lighting my way back to camp. By the time I got there I had no more tears left to cry.

The next night we were marching up into the trenches again along with hundreds of others, to stiffen the line they told us. That could only mean one thing: an attack was expected and we would be in for a packet of trouble. As it turned out, Fritz was to give us a couple of days' grace — no attack came, not yet.

Charlie came instead, just strolled into our dugout as if he'd been gone five minutes. "Afternoon, Tommo. Afternoon, all," he said, grinning from ear to ear. His arrival gave us all new heart. With Sergeant Hanley still on our backs, always on the prowl, we had our champion back, the only one of us who had ever faced him down. As for me, I had my guardian back, my brother and my best friend. Like everyone else I felt suddenly safer.

I was there when Sergeant Hanley and Charlie came face to face in the trench. "What a nice surprise, Sergeant," Charlie chirped. "I heard you'd joined us."

"And I heard you'd been malingering, Peaceful," Hanley snarled. "I don't like malingerers. I've got my eye on you, Peaceful. You're a troublemaker, always have been. I'm warning you, one step out of line . . ."

"Don't you worry yourself, Sergeant," said Charlie. "I'll be good as gold. Cross my heart and hope to die."

The sergeant looked first nonplussed, then explosive.

"Nice weather we're having, Sergeant," Charlie went on. "It's raining in Blighty, you know. Cats and dogs." Hanley pushed past him, muttering to himself as he went. It was a little enough victory, but it cheered all of us who witnessed it to the bottom of our hearts.

That evening Charlie and I sat drinking our tea over a guttering lamp and talked quietly together for the first time. I was full of questions about everyone at home, but he seemed unwilling to say much about them. I was taken aback by this, hurt even, until he saw I was and explained why.

"It's like we're living two separate lives in two separate worlds, Tommo, and I want to keep it that way. I never want the one to touch on the other. I didn't want to bring horrible Hanley and whizzbangs back home, did I? And for me it's the same the other way round. Home's home. Here's here. It's difficult to explain, but little Tommo and Molly, Mother and Big Joe, they don't belong in this hell hole of a place, do they? By talking about them I bring them here, and I don't want to do that. You understand, Tommo?"

And I did.

We hear the shell coming and know from the shriek of it

that it will be close, and it is. The blast of it throws us all to the ground, putting out lamps and plunging us into pungent darkness. It is the first shell of thousands. Our guns answer almost at once, and from then on the titanic duel is almost constant as the world above us erupts, the roar and thunder pounding us remorselessly all day, all night. When the guns do let up it is all the more cruel, for it gives us some fragile hope it might at last be over, only to snatch that hope away again minutes later.

To begin with we huddle together in the dugout and try to pretend to ourselves it isn't happening, and even if it is, that our dugout is deep enough to see us through. We all know in our heart of hearts that a direct hit will be the end of all of us. We know it and accept it. We just prefer not to think about it, and certainly not to talk about it. We drink our tea, smoke our Woodbines, eat when food comes — which isn't often — and go on living as best we can, as normally as we can.

It doesn't seem possible, but on the second day the bombardment intensifies. Every heavy gun the Germans have seems to be aimed at our sector. There is a moment when the last fragile vestiges of controlled fear give way to terror, a terror that can be hidden no longer. I find myself curled into a ball on the ground and screaming for it to stop. Then I feel Charlie lying beside me, folding himself around me to protect me, to comfort me. He begins to sing *Oranges and Lemons* softly in my ear, and soon I am singing with him, and loudly too, singing instead of screaming. Before we know it the whole dugout is singing along with us. But the barrage goes on and on and on, until in the end neither Charlie nor *Oranges and Lemons* can drive away the terror that is engulfing me and invading me, destroying any last glimmer of courage and composure I may have left. All I have now is my fear.

When their attack comes, in the pearly light of dawn, it falters before it even gets near our wire. Our machine gunners see to that, knocking them down like thousands of grey skittles, never to rise again. My hands are shaking so much I can hardly reload my rifle. When they recoil and turn and run we wait for the whistle and then go out over the top. I go because the others go, moving forward as if in a trance, as if outside myself altogether. I find myself suddenly on my knees and I don't know why. There is blood pouring down my face, and my head is wracked with a sudden burning pain so terrible that I feel it must burst. I feel myself falling out of my dream down into a world of swirling darkness. I am being beckoned into a world I have never been to before, where it is warm and comforting and all-enveloping. I know I am dying my own death, and I welcome it.

FIVE TO FIVE

Sixty-five minutes to go. How shall I live them? Shall I try to sleep? It would be useless to try. Should I eat a hearty breakfast? I don't want it. Shall I scream and shout? What would be the point? Shall I pray? Why? What for? Who to?

No. They will do what they will do. Field Marshal Haig is God out here, and Haig has signed. Haig has confirmed the sentence. He has decreed that Private Peaceful will die, will be shot for cowardice in the face of the enemy at six o'clock on the morning of the twenty-fifth of June 1916.

The firing squad will be having their breakfast by now,

sipping their tea, hating what they will have to do. No one has told me where exactly it will happen. I don't want it to be in some dark prison yard with grey walls all around. I want it to be where there is sky and clouds and trees, and birds. It will be easier if there are birds. And let it be quickly over. Please let it be quickly over.

❖ ❖ ❖

I wake to the muffled sound of machine-gun fire, to the distant shriek of the shells. The earth quivers and trembles about me, but I am strangely relieved, for all this must mean that I'm not dead. Nor am I all that alarmed at first when I find that all I can see is darkness, because I remember at once that I have been wounded — I can still feel the throbbing in my head. It must be night and I am lying wounded somewhere in no-man's-land, looking up into the black of the sky. But then I try to move my head a little, and the blackness begins to crumble and fall in on me, filling my mouth, my eyes, my ears. It is not the sky I am looking at, but earth. I feel the weight of it now, pressing down on my chest. My legs cannot move, nor my arms. Only my fingers. How slowly I come to know and understand that I am buried, buried alive, but then how fast I panic. They must have thought I was dead, and buried me, but I am not. I am not! I scream then, and the earth fills my mouth and at once chokes off my breathing. My fingers scrabble, clawing frantically at the earth, but I am suffocating and they cannot help me. I try to think, to calm my raging panic, to try to lie still, to force myself to try to breathe through my nose. But there is no air to breathe. I think of Molly then and commit myself to holding her in my head until the moment I die.

I feel a hand on my leg. One foot is gripped, then the other. From far away I think I hear a voice, and I know it is Charlie's voice. He is calling for me to hang on. They are digging for me, pulling at me, dragging me out into blessed daylight, out into blessed air. I gulp the air like water, choking on it, coughing on it, and then at last I can breathe it in.

The next thing I know I am sitting deep down in what looks like the remains of a concrete dugout, full of exhausted men, all faces I know. Pete is coming down the steps. He is gasping for breath, like me. Charlie is still pouring the last dribbles from his water bottle onto my face, trying to clean me up. "Thought we'd lost you, Tommo," Charlie is saying. "The same shell that buried you killed half a dozen of us. You were lucky. Your head's a bit of a mess. You lie still, Tommo. You've lost a lot of blood." I'm shaking now. I'm cold all over and weak as a kitten.

Pete is crouching beside us now, his forehead pressed

against his rifle. "All hell's broken loose out there," he says. "We're going down like flies, Charlie. They've got us pinned down, machine guns on three sides. Stick your head out of there and you're a dead man."

"Where are we?" I ask.

"Middle of bloody no-man's-land, that's where, some old German dugout," Pete replies. "Can't go forward, can't go back."

"Then we'd best stay put for a while, hadn't we?" Charlie says.

I look up and see Sergeant Hanley standing over us, rifle in hand and shouting at us. "Stay put? Stay put? You listen to me, Peaceful. I give the orders round here. When I say we go, we go. Do I make myself clear?"

Charlie looks him straight in the eye in open defiance and does not look away, just as he used to do with Mr. Munnings at school when he was being ticked off.

"Soon as I give the word," the sergeant goes on, to everyone in the dugout now, "we make a dash for it, and I mean all of us. No stragglers, no malingerers — that means you, Peaceful. Our orders are to press home the attack and then hold our ground. Only fifty yards or so to the German trenches. We'll get there easy."

I wait till the sergeant moves away, until he can't hear. "Charlie," I whisper, "I don't think I can make it. I don't think I can stand up."

"It's all right," he says, and his face breaks into a sudden smile. "You look a right mess, Tommo. All blood and mud, with a couple of little white eyes looking out. Don't you worry, we'll stay together, no matter what. We always have, haven't we?"

The sergeant waits a minute or two by the opening of the dugout until there is a lull in the firing outside. "Right," he says. "This is it. We're going out. Make sure you've all got a full magazine and one up the spout. Everyone ready? On your feet. Let's go." No one moves. The men are looking at one another, hesitating. "What in Hell's name is the matter with you? On your feet, damn you! On your feet!"

Then Charlie speaks up, very quietly. "I think they're thinking what I'm thinking, Sergeant. You take us out there now and their machine guns'll just mow us down. They've seen us go in here, and they'll be waiting for us to come out. They're not stupid. Maybe we should stay here and then go back after dark. No point in going out there and getting ourselves killed for nothing, is there, Sergeant?"

"Are you disobeying my order, Peaceful?" The sergeant is ranting like a man demented now.

"No, I'm just letting you know what I think," Charlie replies. "What we all think."

"And I'm telling you, Peaceful, that if you don't come with us when we go, it won't just be field punishment again. It'll be a court martial for you. It'll be the firing squad. Do you hear me, Peaceful? Do you hear me?"

"Yes, Sergeant," says Charlie. "I hear you. But the thing is, Sergeant, even if I wanted to, I can't go with you because I'd have to leave Tommo behind, and I can't do that. As you can see, Sergeant, he's been wounded. He can hardly walk, let alone run. I'm not leaving him. I'll be staying with him. Don't you worry about us, Sergeant, we'll make our way back later when it gets dark. We'll be all right."

"You miserable little worm, Peaceful." The sergeant is threatening Charlie with his rifle now, the bayonet inches from Charlie's nose and trembling with fury. "I should shoot you right where you are and save the firing squad the trouble." For just a moment it looks as if the sergeant really will do it, but then he remembers himself, and turns away. "You lot, on your feet. On my word, I want you men out there. Make no mistake, it's a court martial for anyone who stays."

One by one the men get unwillingly to their feet, each one preparing himself in his own way, a last drag on a cigarette, a silent prayer, eyes closed.

"Go! Go! Go!" The sergeant is screaming, and they do go, leaping up the steps of the dugout and dashing out into the open. I hear the German machine guns opening up again. Pete is the last to leave the dugout. He pauses on the step and looks back down at us. "You should come, Charlie," he says. "He means it. The bastard means what he says, I promise you."

"I know he does," says Charlie. "So do I. G'luck, Pete. Keep your head down."

Then Pete is gone and we're alone together in the dugout. We don't need to imagine what is going on out there. We can hear it, the screams cut short, the death rattle of machine guns, the staccato of rifle fire picking them off one by one. Then it goes quiet and we wait. I look across at Charlie. I see there are tears in his eyes. "Poor beggars," he says. "Poor beggars." And then: "I think I've cooked my goose good and proper this time, Tommo."

"Maybe the sergeant won't come back," I tell him.

"Let's hope," says Charlie. "Let's hope."

I must have drifted in and out of consciousness after that. Each time I woke I saw that another one or two had made it back to the dugout, but still no Sergeant Hanley. Still I hoped. Then I woke to find myself lying with Charlie's arm around me, my head resting on his shoulder.

"Tommo? Tommo?" he said. "You awake?"

"Yes," I said.

"Listen Tommo, I've been thinking. If the worst happens —"

"It's not going to happen," I interrupted.

"Just listen, Tommo, will you? I want you to promise me you'll look after things for me. You understand what I'm saying? You promise?"

"Yes," I said.

Then after a long silence he went on: "You still love her, don't you? You still love Molly?" My silence was enough. He knew already. "Good," said Charlie. "And there's something else I want you to look after too." He lifted his arm away from behind me, took off his watch, and strapped it on my wrist. "There you are, Tommo. It's a wonderful watch, this. Never stopped, not once. Don't lose it." I didn't know what to say. "Now you can go back to sleep again," he said.

And in my sleep I dreamt again my childhood nightmare, Father's finger pointing at me, and I promised myself, even as I dreamt, that when I woke this time I would at last tell Charlie what I did in that forest all those years ago.

I opened my eyes. Sergeant Hanley was sitting across the dugout from us, looking at us darkly from under his helmet. As we waited for the others to come in and for darkness to fall, the sergeant sat there not saying another word to Charlie or to anyone, just glaring unwaveringly at Charlie. There was cold hate in his eyes.

By nightfall there was still no sign of Pete, nor of a dozen others who'd gone out with the sergeant to join that futile charge. The sergeant decided it was time to go. So in the dark of the night, by twos and threes, the remnants of the company crawled back to our trenches across no-man's-land, Charlie half dragging me, half lifting me all the way. From my stretcher in the bottom of the trench I looked up and saw Charlie being taken away under close arrest. It all happened so fast after that. There was no time for goodbyes. Only when he'd gone did I remember again my dream and the promise I'd made in it, and had not kept.

They did not let me see him again for another six weeks, and by then the court martial was all over, the death sentence passed and then confirmed. That was all I knew, all anyone knew. I knew nothing whatever of how it had all happened until yesterday, when at last I was allowed to see him. They were holding him at Walker Camp. The guard outside said he was sorry, but I had only twenty minutes. Orders, he said.

It is a stable — and it still smells like it — with a table and two chairs, a bucket in the corner, and a bed along one wall. Charlie is lying on his back, hands under his head, legs crossed. He sits up as soon as he sees me, and smiles broadly. "I hoped you'd come, Tommo," he says. "I didn't think they'd let you. How's your head? All mended?"

"Good as new," I tell him, trying to respond in kind to his cheeriness. And then we're standing there hugging one another, and I can't help myself.

"I want no tears, Tommo," he whispers in my ear. "This is going to be difficult enough without tears." He holds me at arm's length. "Understand?"

I can do no more than nod.

He has had a letter from home, from Molly, which he must read out to me, he says, because it makes him laugh and he needs to laugh. It's mostly about little Tommo. Molly writes that he's already learning to blow raspberries and they're every bit as loud and rude as ours when we were young. And she says Big Joe sings him to sleep at night, *Oranges and Lemons* of course. She ends by sending her love and hoping we're both well.

"Doesn't she know?" I ask.

"No," Charlie" says. "And they won't know, not until afterwards. They'll send them a telegram. They didn't let me write home until today." As we sit down at the table he lowers his voice and we talk in half-whispers now. "You'll tell them how it really was, won't you, Tommo? It's all I care about now. I don't want them thinking I was a coward. I don't want that. I want them to know the truth."

"Didn't you tell the court martial?" I ask him.

"Course I did. I tried, I tried my very best, but there's none so deaf as them that don't want to hear. They had their one witness, Sergeant Hanley, and he was all they needed. It wasn't a trial, Tommo. They'd made up their minds I was guilty before they even sat down. I had three of them, a brigadier and two captains looking down their noses at me as if I was some sort of dirt. I told them everything, Tommo, just like it happened. I had nothing to be ashamed of, did I? I wasn't going to hide anything. So I told them that, yes, I did disobey the sergeant's order because the order was stupid, suicidal — we all knew it was — and that anyway I had to stay behind to look after you. They knew a dozen or more got wiped out in the attack, that no one even got as far as the German wire. They knew I was right, but it made no difference."

"What about witnesses?" I ask him. "You should have had witnesses. I could have said. I could have told them."

"I asked for you, Tommo, but they wouldn't accept you because you were my brother. I asked for Pete, but then they told me that Pete was missing. And as for the rest of the company, I was told they'd been moved into another sector, and were up in the line and not available. So they heard it all from Sergeant Hanley, and they swallowed everything he told them, like it was gospel truth, I think there's a big push coming, and they wanted to make an example of someone, Tommo. And I was the Charlie." He laughed at that. "A right Charlie. Then of course there was my record as a troublemaker — 'a mutinous troublemaker,' Hanley called me. Remember Etaples? Had up on a charge of gross insubordination? Field Punishment Number One? It was all there on my record. So was my foot."

"Your foot?"

"That time I was shot in the foot. All foot wounds are suspicious, they said. It could have been self-inflicted — it goes on all the time, they said. I could have done it myself, just to get myself out of the trenches and back to Blighty."

"But it wasn't like that," I say.

"Course it wasn't. They believed what they wanted to believe."

"Didn't you have anyone to speak up for you?" I ask him. "Like an officer or someone?"

"I didn't think I needed one," Charlie tells me. "Just tell them the truth, Charlie, and you'll be all right. That's what I thought. How wrong could I be? I thought maybe a letter of good character from Wilkie would help. I was sure they'd listen to him, him being an officer and one of them. I told them where I thought he was. The last I'd heard he was up in a hospital in Scotland somewhere. They told me they'd written to the hospital, but that he'd died of his wounds six months before. The whole court martial took less than an hour, Tommo. That's all they gave me. An hour for a man's life. Not a lot, is it? And do you know what the brigadier said, Tommo? He said I was a worthless man. Worthless. I've been called a lot of things in my life, Tommo, but none of them ever upset me, except that one. I didn't show it, mind. I wouldn't have given them the satisfaction. And then he passed sentence. I was expecting it by then. Didn't upset me nearly as much as I thought it would."

I hang my head, because I cannot stop my eyes filling.

"Tommo," he says, lifting my chin. "Look on the bright side. It's no more than we were facing every day in the trenches. It'll be over very quick. And the boys are looking after me all right here. They don't like it any more than I do. Three hot meals a day. A man can't grumble. It's all over and done with, or it will be soon anyway. You want some tea, Tommo? They brought me some just before you came."

So we sit either side of the table and share a mug of sweet, strong tea, and speak of everything Charlie wants to talk about: home, bread-and-butter pudding with the raisins in it and the crunchy crust on top, moonlit nights fishing for sea trout on the Colonel's river, Bertha, beer at The Duke, the yellow airplane and the humbugs.

"We won't talk of Big Joe or Mother or Moll," Charlie says, "because I'll cry if I do, and I promised myself I wouldn't." He leant forward suddenly in great earnest, clutching my hand. "Talking of promises, that promise you made me back in the dugout. Tommo, You won't forget it, will you? You will look after them?"

"I promise," I tell him, and I've never meant anything so much in all my life.

"You've still got the watch then," he says, pulling back my sleeve. "Keep it ticking for me, and then when the time comes, give it to Little Tommo, so he'll have something from me. I'd like that. You'll make him a good father, like Father was to us."

It is the moment. I have to do it now. It is my last chance. I tell him about how Father had died, about how it had happened, what I had done, how I should have told him years ago, but had never dared to. He smiles. "I always knew that, Tommo. So did Mother. You'd talk in your sleep. Always having nightmares, always keeping me awake about it, you were. All nonsense. Not your fault. It was the tree that killed Father, Tommo, not you."

"You sure?" I ask him.

"I'm sure," he says. "Quite sure."

We look at one another and know that time is getting short now. I see a flicker of panic in his eyes. He pulls some letters out of his pocket and pushes them across the table. "You'll see they get these, Tommo?"

We grip hands across the table, put our foreheads together and close our eyes. I manage to say what I've been wanting to say.

"You're not worthless, Charlie. They're the worthless bastards. You're the best friend I've ever had, the best person I've ever known."

I hear Charlie starting to hum softly. It is *Oranges and Lemons*, slightly out of tune. I hum with him, our hands clasping tighter, our humming stronger now. Then we are singing, singing it out loud so that the whole world can hear us, and we are laughing as we sing. And there are tears, but it does not matter because these are not tears of sadness, they are tears of celebration. When we've finished, Charlie says: "It's what I'll be singing in the morning. It won't be God Save the ruddy King or All Things bleeding Bright and Beautiful. It'll be *Oranges and Lemons* for Big Joe, for all of us."

The guard comes in and tells us our time is up. We shake hands then, as strangers do. There are no words left to say. I hold our last look and want to hold it forever. Then I turn away and leave him.

When I got back to camp yesterday afternoon I expected the sympathy and the long faces and all those averted eyes I'd been used to for days before. Instead I was greeted by smiles and with the news that Sergeant Hanley was dead. He had been killed, they told me, in a freak accident, blown up by a grenade out on the ranges. So there was some justice, of a sort, but it had come too late for Charlie. I hoped someone at Walker Camp had heard about it and would tell Charlie. It would be small consolation for him, but it would be something. Any jubilation I felt, or any of us felt, turned very soon to grim satisfaction, and then evaporated completely. It seemed as if the entire regiment was subdued, like me; quite unable to think of anything else but Charlie, of the injustice he was suffering, and the inevitability of what must happen to him in the morning.

We have been billeted this last week or so around an empty farmhouse, less than a mile down the road from where they're keeping Charlie at Walker Camp. We've been waiting to go up into the trenches further down the line on the Somme. We live in bell tents, and the officers are billeted in the house. The others have been doing their very best to make it as easy as they can for me. I know from their every look how much they feel for me, NCOs and officers too. But kind though they are I do not want or need their sympathy or their help. I do not even want the distraction of their company. I want simply to be alone. Late in the evening I take a lamp with me and move out of the tent into this barn, or what is left of it. They bring me blankets and food, and then leave me to myself. They understand. The padre comes to do what he can. He can do nothing. I send him away. So here I am now with the night gone so fast and the clock ticking towards six o'clock. When the time comes, I will go outside, and I will look up at the sky because I know Charlie will be doing the same as they take him out. We'll be seeing the same clouds, feeling the same breeze on our faces. At least that way we'll be together.

ONE MINUTE
TO SIX

I try to close my mind to what is happening this minute to Charlie. I try just to think of Charlie as he was at home, as we all were. But all I can see in my mind are the soldiers leading Charlie out into the field. He is not stumbling. He is not struggling. He is not crying out. He is walking with his head held high, just as he was after Mr. Munnings caned him at school that day. Maybe there's a lark rising, or a great crow wheeling into the wind above him. The firing squad stands at ease, waiting. Six men, their rifles loaded and ready, each one wanting only to get it over with. They will be shooting one of their own, and it feels to them like murder. They try not to look at Charlie's face.

Charlie is tied to the post. The padre says a prayer, makes the sign of the cross on his forehead and moves away. It is cold now but Charlie does not shiver. The officer, his revolver drawn, is looking at his watch. They try to put a hood over Charlie's head, but he will not have it. He looks up to the sky and sends his last living thoughts back home.

"Present! Ready! Aim!"

He closes his eyes and as he waits he sings softly. *"Oranges and Lemons, say the bells of St. Clements."* Under my breath I sing it with him. I hear the echoing volley. It is done. It is over. With that volley a part of me has died with him. I turn back to go to the solitude of my hay barn, and I find I am far from alone in my grieving. All over the camp I see them standing to attention outside their tents. And the birds are singing.

❖   ❖   ❖

I am not alone that afternoon either when I go to Walker Camp to collect his belongings, and to see where they have buried him. He would like the place. He looks out over a water meadow down to where a brook runs softly under the trees. They tell me he walked out with a smile on his face as if he were going for an early-morning stroll. They tell me that he refused the hood, and that they thought he was singing when he died. Six of us who were in the dugout that day stand vigil over his grave until sundown. Each of us says the same thing when we leave.

"Bye, Charlie."

The next day the regiment is marching up the road towards the Somme. It is late June, and they say there's soon going to be an almighty push and we're going to be part of it. We'll push them all the way to Berlin. I've heard that before. All I know is that I must survive. I have promises to keep.

POSTSCRIPT

In the First World War, between 1914 and 1918, over 290 soldiers of the British and Commonwealth armies were executed by firing squad, some for desertion and cowardice, two for simply sleeping at their posts.

Many of these men we now know were traumatized by shell shock. Court martials were brief, the accused often unrepresented.

To this day the injustice they suffered has never been officially recognized. The British government continues to refuse to grant posthumous pardons.

❖   ❖   ❖

AUTHOR'S NOTE

From 1914–1918, the great European powers were locked in the most self-destructive war the world has ever known. The armies fought themselves to a standstill in the mud of Belgium and northern France, and dug themselves into defensive positions that stretched from the Swiss border in the east to the English Channel in the west.

For four terrible years millions of soldiers hurled themselves at one another, the German army on the one side, the Allied armies (primarily British, French, and Belgian) on the other. It became a war of attrition, of murderous bombardments and futile attacks, with men as expendable as munitions.

Gas and tanks were used for the first time as weapons of war. In one day alone, July 1st, 1916, the British army lost 60,000 (killed and wounded).

The stalemate and slaughter was only ended after the United States entered the war on the Allied side in 1917. This tipped the balance, and after one last, desperate German offensive, the Germans sued for peace. An armistice was signed at 11 o'clock on the 11th day on the 11th month of 1918. Over ten million men had died in the conflict, including 40,000 Americans.

Many years ago I came to learn of this war, not from history books, but from the men who fought in it. I met and talked to three old veterans from my village of Iddesleigh, in Devon, England. They spoke movingly, hauntingly of the terrors they had lived through, of the comrades they had lost. As a consequence I was inspired to write *War Horse*, the story of a farm horse taken from the village to be a cavalry horse in that dreadful war. It is the story of the war, on both sides, as seen through the eyes of the horse.

Then, and subsequently, I have made many research trips to the battlefields of Belgium and France. During one of these visits five years ago, I discovered that over 300 British soldiers had been executed, shot at dawn, for cowardice or desertion, with two for sleeping at their posts. I read their stories, studied their trials, and saw the telegrams sent to their mothers. I visited the places where they had been shot. I stood over their graves.

That a shameful injustice had been done to these unfortunate men seemed to me beyond doubt. Their judges called them "worthless." Their trials, or court martials, were brief, under twenty minutes in some cases. Twenty minutes for a man's life. Often they had no one to speak for them and no witnesses were called in their defense. There was, I felt, a presumption of guilt. We know now, as they knew then, that most of these men were traumatized by shell shock. When their ends came it was always at dawn, and often they were shot by a firing squad made up of unwilling friends and comrades. The youngest soldier to be executed was just seventeen.

Successive British governments have since refused to acknowledge the injustice suffered by these men, and have refused to grant posthumous pardons — which would of course be a great consolation to surviving relatives. The New Zealand government have pardoned their executed soldiers; it can be done. The Australians and the Americans, to their credit, never allowed their soldiers to be executed in the first place.

The more I thought about it, the more I knew I had to tell the story of these men. *Private Peaceful* (a name taken from a gravestone I discovered in a cemetery in Belgium) is a fictional story, but it is drawn from many true stories. He is one of these men, all of these men. To live with them, with him, through the last night of his life, seemed to me to be a way of coming closer to how it must have been for them, a way of understanding more about what is worthless and what is not, about courage and cowardice, a way of understanding more about ourselves.

— MICHAEL MORPURGO
Iddesleigh
October 2003